DEATH'S BLOODY TRAIL

"Who are you?" Shin gasped. "What do you want?"

"A butcher, a baker, a candlestick maker," the shrouded figure before him said drily.

"What are you talking about?" Shin cried shrilly, his voice getting louder.

"When your restaurant burned," said the Ninja softly, "why were all the exit doors padlocked shut? Why was the emergency water supply turned off? And why weren't you there on the busiest night of the week?"

"I . . . I don't know!" Shin babbled as he backed away.

Brett Wallace sliced a two-inch opening on Shin's jawline with the sharp edge of his kamayari. "Now do you know?" the Ninja calmly asked.

"Oh God, help! Help me!" Shin screamed. His bodyguards came on the run, scrambling toward the sound of their employer's voice while pulling 9mm automatics from their shoulder holsters.

The kamayari spun in Brett Wallace's hand as he turned to face them. . .

Books by Wade Barker

Ninja Master #1: Vengeance Is His

Ninja Master #2: Mountain of Fear

Ninja Master #3: Borderland of Hell

Ninja Master #4: Million-Dollar Massacre

Ninja Master #5: Black Magician

Ninja Master #6: Death's Door

Ninja Master #7: The Skin Swindle

Ninja Master #8: Only The Good Die

Published by
WARNER BOOKS

NINJA MASTER

#8
ONLY
THE
GOOD
DIE

Wade Barker

WARNER BOOKS

A Warner Communications Company

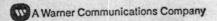 A Warner Communications Company

Printed in the United States of America

First Printing: May, 1983

10 9 8 7 6 5 4 3 2 1

To all the friendly associates at the company:
Jim, Ed, Nansey, and Brian . . .
"Arrigato"

NINJA MASTER

#8
ONLY
THE
GOOD
DIE

Chapter One

The dead had one thing in common, and it wasn't their murderer.

It wasn't their sex, it wasn't their skin color, and it wasn't their age. It wasn't any of the things police might be able to string together for motive. Pure and simple, it was the fact that none deserved to die. Not like that. Not like Tamara Anderson.

"You're not going out like that," her mother said from the kitchen door.

Tamara stopped dead in her tracks, her hand reaching for the front doorknob. She looked over her shoulder, her expression a mixture of guilt with impatience.

"Like what?" she asked, as if daring her mother to tell her.

The older woman was striding across the worn living room rug with impressive vigor even before the words got out of her daughter's mouth. Her boney hand snapped out and clamped on Tamara's stretched tube-top like metal pinchers.

"Don't give me none of your lip," she said, swinging her other hand across Tamara's cheek almost unconsciously. "You know like what."

Tamara's own hands came up too slowly. She heard the sharp slap of old bones against her smooth flesh

9

before she felt the slight stinging pain she had grown accustomed to long before. The old battle-ax is always a lot faster, she thought—no matter how many years and inches separated them.

Although Tamara was only fifteen, she already could look down on her mother, but only in height. It was no great feat since the old woman was five-one, but what her mother lacked in stature, she made up in strength. She had to. No black woman in New York could survive with four children and no husband without a firm backbone and fast hands.

The old woman's hand pulled the tank top away from Tamara's chest, freeing her strong, well-developed breasts —the pride of PS 182 in Harlem. All the girls were envious of her blossoming figure, not to mention the attention the boys paid.

Tamara's right arm came up late, but better than never, knocking her mother's claw away. The elastic tube snapped back over the dark mounds, slapping her septum. She backed away toward her room while her mother moved forward to block the door.

"I don't care," the young girl screeched. "It's hot."

"No daughter of mine is going out into the streets looking like that," the old woman said with resolve. "Even if it's two hundred degrees. You go change."

As often as the attacks had come, Tamara was still unable to protect herself. Somehow the biddy always managed to get under her defensives. But someday . . . someday she'd catch the monster's old wings in midair, and then nothing would keep her from doing what she wanted to do.

"Ma," Tamara wailed, the voice rising up like a siren. "Aaron is waiting for me!"

"Then, he'll just have to wait a little longer," the mother replied firmly. She must have said the same thing at least a hundred thousand times in her life. The words were now like old friends—ones Mrs. Anderson made comfortable whenever they visited. "Go change. Now. Where'd you get that thing anyway?"

Tamara clamped her lips shut. She wanted to go at it tooth and nail, but she wasn't prepared. Her mother couldn't keep her in, but she could make life hell for her. Especially since she had borrowed the tube-top from Roseann upstairs. And as soon as she thought of her, Tamara heard in her mind's ear the screaming fights Roseann and her mother always had.

The whole apartment complex couldn't help but hear the battle royals Roseann and her mom had at least three times a week—if not a night. Tamara was just at that age where she'd be willing to take on her own mom, but she remembered how embarrassing and stupid Roseann sounded, as well as her own vow never to become like her friend.

So Tamara's lips tightened, her fists clenched, and she whirled around. Deciding to ignore her mother, she stalked back to her room, fuming. She marched silently into the small enclosure and tried to slam the thin hollow-frame door shut. Since it was so light it caught the air and, pitifully, closed very slowly.

Once separated from her nemesis, Tamara relaxed and looked on the bright side. At least this would keep her ma from getting too upset about her next change of clothes. She went to her simple, sagging bed, reached underneath, and pulled out the large cardboard chest.

Resting on her knees, she pulled off the tube-top over her head, exposing her chest in a sort of triumph. To her delight her newly growing breasts stood at attention. Now *that* is what she called black pride. Her happy mood was broken by snickering coming from the dirty, open window.

She looked up with no surprise to see her little brother staring at her and giggling. He was laughing both at her exhibitionism and at her loss to the mouth of their mother. She raised the tube-top in her fist, then thought

11

better of it. If Michael got his hands on it, there's no telling what she'd have to do to get it back. And she was late enough as it was.

She quickly changed to the accompaniment of her nine-year-old brother's laughter. Off came the skintight jeans. Off came the sandals. On went an aqua leotard top over her frizzy mane of black curly hair. On went some dark shorts, and a pair of sneakers. Tamara was pleased. This outfit, if anything, was even worse than the other. Now, in addition to breasts, there were legs.

Tamara stood tall, basking in her pubescent glory as Michael was hit with a new paroxysm of mirth. As she walked back toward the doorway to the living room, she tied a rolled silk scarf around her head like a headband.

The door had not closed all the way. Tamara looked through the crack to find her mother back in the kitchen. She waited breathlessly until the old woman looked away from her door.

She was about to make a break for the front door when she heard the unmistakeable call of Mrs. Morris from across the way. To her it was like a call from the governor just as the switch was about to be pulled. That crone would have her mother gossiping across the alleyway for hours.

Tamara immediately loped across the living room. With practiced ease she twisted and pulled open all four locks in less than three seconds. One more twist and pull, then she was out. She was already striding down the hall before the door closed on her mother's shout.

"Tamara!"

She couldn't afford to wait for the wheezing, creaky old elevator and she didn't want to have a confrontation in the hall for everyone to hear, so she pushed open the stairwell door. She took the steps like a practiced long-distance runner. She was already a flight below when her mother burst onto the landing.

"Tamara, you come back here this instant!"

"It's all right, ma," she called merrily back, unknowingly paraphrasing Bob Dylan. "I'll be home later."

"You come here right now or I might not let you come back!" the old woman shouted. It was a threat she would come to forever regret.

"Then, I won't come back," Tamara said, still trotting down the steps.

"Tamara!"

"See you later, ma."

The girl pushed open the heavy lobby floor door and skipped across the cracked, faded tile of the entrance hall. The area was awash with the heady gold of sunset, which blinded her as she headed for the front doors.

She could finally see the magnificently colored clouds clearly as she walked down the grafitti-strewn concrete path of the housing development. Orange and red highlights were painted across the cumulus bottoms, framed by a dark purple line. It was amazing that nature allowed such beauty even in Harlem. Tamara breathed deeply of it and her freedom, feeling the tension across her shoulders and brow lighten. This is how the slaves must have felt after the Emancipation Proclamation, she thought.

The same old bunch sat in cliques around the fenced entranceway to the low-income housing complex, and they hooted at the sight of her. The younger ones made the usual amount of noise while the codgers made greetings as well as warnings.

"Looking good, mama!"

"Hey, what you say, little sister?"

"Whoo-wee, baby-girl, where'd you come from?"

"You gonna get a bad burn in this heat, darlin'."

Tamara smiled inwardly, keeping up a show of outward indifference. Those guys were all right. They kept things cool. Over the years they had become kind of like palace guards, making sure the wrong kind of people didn't come in and the wrong kind of things didn't go on. They knew that just one slip could turn the place into a zoo or a jail. They had seen enough places go that way. So they banded together to make sure the same thing didn't happen here.

Tamara left the stringent security of the complex behind, mingling with the rest of the evening crowd. In Manhattan's mid-summer, darkness came late in the day. The girl was skirting on the line between day and night even though it was almost eight-thirty. She looked around. Everywhere were black faces wearing next to nothing in the ninety-degree heat. Some of the outfits made her running/exercise uniform look like a nun's habit.

She felt better and kept on feeling better as she neared the rendezvous point. It might have been strange to anyone who lived on the other side of 110th Street, but she never felt frightened on the streets. Everybody knew her in the neighborhood, and she knew everybody. And they all watched out for each other.

Aaron and she liked a little privacy, which was in short supply as the weather got hotter. But they had found a spot in the mouth of an alley between deserted factory and a closed-down gas station.

The gas station was put out of business by the fuel shortage in the late seventies and stayed closed as the vandals made quick work of the place. The local factory had bottled mineral and seltzer water for decades until Perrier became all the rage. To this day Tamara found it funny that clean mountain water ever came out of Harlem.

She grinned at the factory's faded sign as she neared the meeting place. The traffic on both the street and sidewalk thinned as she approached. The spot was sandwiched between two busy intersections. Once cars got on one, they rarely saw any reason to switch to the other, so their makeshift lover's lane was fairly deserted.

As she rounded the corner she heard Aaron's tape

14

player pumping out funkadelic at a low volume. It was about as romantic as he got. He kept the volume low because he didn't want to attract much attention, but he kept the bass high because he loved the beat. He smiled as she came into view.

Tamara returned the smile, liking what she saw. What she saw was a tall, thin young black in a T-shirt, black polyester pants, and dirty white sneakers. The silver ghetto-blaster was resting on an empty oil drum next to him. She glanced behind her. The roadway and sidewalk were empty. The street lights had yet to come on.

"Hey babe," Aaron said, moving forward and wrapping an arm around her waist. "What took you?" He sat back on a box, pulled her toward him, and aimed one at her mouth. He kissed her cheek as she moved her face aside and planted her palms against his chest.

"Nice," she breathed, putting her own arm around his neck. She put her knee on the box top between his legs and moved her lips in line with his. The next kiss was on target. After that she needed no excuse for tardiness.

"Hungry?" he asked when they had finally disentangled.

"You know it," she said, keeping the double meaning intact.

He put an arm around her shoulder and started marching toward the alley mouth. "The others'll be meeting us at the White Castle," he said. "We can see what's doin' from there."

She nodded, smiling up at him. But her smile faltered when his eyes clouded over and his hand touched his chest. Only then did she hear the cough.

"Aaron, you all right?" she asked. His head turned toward her, and one side of his mouth smiled. It gave him a confused, sick expression. He suddenly looked up, and she heard another cough.

"Something stuck in your throat?" she asked with only a slight bit of urgency. "What's the matter?"

15

Aaron stopped walking, and one leg moved back. Tamara heard a third cough, and then Aaron dropped to his knees.

His arm was still around her shoulder, so he dragged her with him. She kneeled beside him on her toes, as her right arm went around his back to support him and her left hand settled over the one he held to his chest.

"What is it?" Tamara asked the glassy-eyed, open-mouthed face. She felt something wet on his fingers. Instinctively she knew it wasn't sweat. She drew her hand away. Her fingertips were coated with liquid.

Her eyes went from her hand to his torso. The darkness had cloaked the wounds, but not enough so she couldn't see the spreading stains across his cotton-covered chest. She was about to speak again when she felt him stop breathing. She actually sensed that his heart had stopped beating through the arm across his back.

Tamara stared in shock as Aaron's corpse slid from beneath her grip and fell on his side.

The girl slipped to her knees. Both fists came up into her widening mouth to choke off the cry of fear. She would have been wiser to scream. Because as her eyes filled with tears, she heard what her mind later automatically identified as running footsteps and two hands gripped her throat like a vise.

The hands tightened, and the arms behind them pushed, keeping her on bended knees as she weakly struggled. Her writhing became stronger as she vaguely heard the voices.

"Incredible," said one. Low, but clear. "He's dead all right."

"I told you," said the other from behind Tamara. "Frank can practically slip those shells underneath the skin without them feeling it. Give me a hand with this one, will you?"

The girl looked up in time to see a dark-clothed figure

16

approaching her from Aaron's corpse. Panic pushed her struggling to new heights, but the men who held her reacted as if she were only a frisky puppy.

"That's it," said the one choking her. "Grab her hands." His own hands were crushing her throat, trapping any words she had left in her larynx. She couldn't scream, and she could hardly breathe.

Without any instruction the other had plucked her waving hands out of the air. He waited until her arms came near his own hovering limbs, then snatched her wrists as if grabbing a slow fly.

Suddenly all the fingers left her throat. She wanted to scream, but her body automatically overrode that instruction to suck in as much air as possible. By the time she was ready to shout, a forearm had slammed across her neck. Another one pressed brutally against her stomach. The air was choked off again.

All she could do was whine as the men lifted her off the ground and dragged her toward the alley entrance. Blocking her view of the street was a dark Lincoln Continental. It was idling on the sidewalk, it's back door open. To Tamara's panicked mind, it looked like the yawning mouth of hell, with frightful demons waiting to torture her. She had no idea how right her frenzied imagination was.

She wrenched and pulled in their grip, but couldn't get her hands free. Her legs kicked out, hitting next to nothing. Whenever she did manage to connect, her soft sneakers and her attackers' moving legs deflected the blow.

It took them two seconds to get her to the car. They threw her in without ceremony, piling in after her. Her one shout was cut off by the slamming of the door and the roaring of the engine. A moment later the big car was moving down the street, its engine growling with a throaty roar.

"Keep her low," said the driver as the girl struggled

on the laps of the three men in the back seat. The two who had captured her now held her wrists and ankles. The third was pushing a rubber prod deep into her mouth.

"What for?" asked the man in the passenger seat as he started taking his rifle apart. "The windows are opaque." Sure enough, all the windows looked black from the outside.

"Yeah, idiot," the driver replied with mirth. "But the windshield isn't." He snorted. "You may be a great shot, but I don't think your corn bread has risen all the way."

"Hell," said the other, "didn't I tell you? This baby can kill at fifty yards, and they'll never know what hit 'em." He unscrewed the large silencer from the Charter Arms "Explorer" .22 rifle.

The driver shrugged as he turned onto Roosevelt Drive. "I never would have believed you could get that much stopping power and accuracy with a .22—especially with a silencer."

"Don't believe it?" said the gunman, nodding toward the back seat. "Just look at the catch."

The driver took a second to check out their victim. Each man in the back seat had made his professional contribution to her captivity. Dave had pushed the electroshock therapy gag into the girl's mouth and secured it behind her head. Steve had clicked the handcuffs on her wrists behind her back. And Tony had secured her ankles to her thighs with thin belts.

Tamara was sitting on the floor hump, the top of her head just below the front seat back. Steve had his black military knife against her throat, and his other hand in her hair. He was whispering in her ear just as the driver turned his attention back to the roads heading for New England.

"Jesus, Steve," the driver complained, "can't you wait?"

The knife man looked up. "What for? She's ready as she'll ever be."

"The less time we keep her, the better off we'll be," Tony chimed in. "Might as well get a head start. Once we get back, there's no telling how long the others will take."

"Get a head start," chuckled Dave. "I like that."

"Well then, get a move on," said the driver. "We'll be getting to a tollbooth in about twenty minutes."

The casual conversation was enough to truly frighten the girl for the first time. Before, she had been confused. Now she had the time to understand what was happening to her. She could tell from the way they were speaking, the men had as much respect for her as a side of beef.

"No problem," said Steve. "Plenty of time."

He went back to telling her exactly what he was going to do and what she should do with it. The driver heard the sound of a zipper opening. He looked in the rearview mirror. The knife was back at the girl's throat. He heard her choking on the gag's rubber shaft as tears rolled down her face. He saw her shoulders moving as her hands jerked in rhythm.

The driver shook his head in sympathy, vowing that as soon as they got home, he'd be the first to get his piece and get it over with. Frank was too busy packing away the rest of the collapsible Explorer rifle, but Dave didn't see any reason to wait.

While the girl was following Steve's instructions—her manacled hands in his lap—he reached forward and pulled the left side of her leotard down off her breast. What was she doing to Steve he did to her chest; the knife still held tightly against her neck. More than once she thought of pushing herself on the blade, but everytime she tried, the pain pushed her back.

Tony managed to wait until Steve was finished, the result smearing the back of Tamara's leotard. "All right, already, that's enough!" he barked, pushing her off the car hump. Unable to brace herself, the girl fell sideways on the floor, her head hitting Dave's shoes.

"Give me that," Tony demanded, snatching the knife out of Steve's hand. "Now let's get to the nitty gritty."

"Hey, come on!" said the driver. "We'll be at the toll any minute!"

"The way Tony does it, that'll be more than enough time," Dave quipped.

"I didn't notice you taking it easy on her tit," Tony snapped, pulling at Tamara's shorts and bringing the knife down.

"Everything in moderation," Dave soothed smugly.

The girl howled in hysteria as the man sliced and tore away her pants. But the electroshock gag was made to keep mental patients from swallowing their tongues and making any noise that might disturb others. So while it kept her tongue down, it kept her mouth open wide: making it nearly impossible to make any sound louder than a gasp.

The howl turned into a long gurgle that died before it reached the windows. Tony twisted her onto her back and ripped the last piece of cloth away from her legs. The leotard had ridden up high between her legs. He spread her bound legs as wide as they could go by pushing her knees apart and then jammed his own body in between.

Steve and Dave moved their feet up onto the seat with mock grumbles. Although they acted irritated, their eyes were glistening and glued to the floor. Even Frank was staring in anticipation since he had stashed his beloved rifle safely away.

Tamara's hips were resting on the uprisen car hump. Her chin was pushed onto her chest. Her eyes were squeezed shut, and she maintained one long scream, which sounded like a hum that was swallowed up by the thrumming noise of the Lincoln.

Tony pushed his pants down. He grabbed the leotard bottom and brought the knife forward. He cut the last remaining obstruction away. He immediately leaped back in disgust.

"Fuck!" he screamed. "The bitch just shit on me!"

The men roared with laughter as Tony beat the black girl to death.

Chapter Two

No one deserves to die like that. Not like Tamara Anderson and not like Alice Lieberman.

Walking in high heels was never fun, but walking on the hard floors of Grand Central Station was really tough. Sometimes after a busy day she could feel the taut vibrations shooting up her legs with every step. On the outside she may have looked cool and serene—the very picture of the ambitious female executive—but on the inside she knew it was a very loose guise, just barely held together by large doses of Lavoris, Dial, Sure, L'eggs, Clairol, and Saks Fifth Avenue.

"Alice!" She heard her name, but ignored it. It was just one of many sounds the train station belched out in the dull roar it always seemed filled with. For all she knew it might have been shouted by one of the sleeping bums who was having a Lewis Carroll nightmare. Instead she kept her concentration on the entry to her train platform: number 109—the local train from Manhattan to Stamford, Connecticut.

It would be a pleasure to get back home to New Canaan. She'd park her BMW under her condominium window, turn on some Herbert Laws, chill a nice half-bottle of wine and run the bath. After a nice leisurely soak, she'd cuddle into her full-length terry cloth robe, turn the air conditioner to high, stretch out on the couch and luxuriate.

"Alice!" She heard the voice call out again. Boy, she thought, that bum must be riding the White Rabbit hard. That's what he gets for drinking so much of the stuff that makes you small. She continued to ignore the call, looking to her right instead. There it was: the thing she had been dreading all afternoon—the L'Eclair Shoppe.

Why couldn't they move the 5:09 p.m. train to a track opposite a bookstore? Or better yet, one of those hot dog stands. The smell of that roasting mystery meat combined with sauerkraut would be enough to put her off her feed for the rest of the night. But no, instead she had to stare right down the maw of cream, cake, nuts, and fruit.

For a second she was tempted. But one look at the long line of patrons inside was enough to deter her. And another look down at the flat stomach beneath her thin white shirt under the light suit jacket was enough to eliminate the temptation completely. She had worked too long and too hard on those muscles to let a napoleon or cheesecake work their insidious charms on it.

A hand fell on her shoulder. She whirled around powered by a surprised start. Standing before her was Saul Bechner, the office underachiever. "Alice," he said breathlessly.

She recognized the voice now. Sure, it had to be Saul's innocuous voice, full of hope and destined for failure. No wonder she didn't respond. Ever since he had the Fremont Egg account pulled out from under him, he never had been the same. Everybody knew he was just holding on now—his spirit broken, his talents waning.

And everyone knew the longer he held on, the worse it would get until he'd force the company to fire him when his original ability was irretrievable. In the meantime the employees tolerated him. They all listened impatiently to his lunch time and coffee break hopes and scorned his inter-office attempts to consolidate his position.

In the Madison Avenue war he was already listed as D.O.A. And the worst thing of all, he must have known it. Alice pitied Bechner, but she didn't sympathize. She couldn't allow herself that emotion. There, but for the grace of the company, go I, she thought.

Now he only made her uncomfortable. She dreaded meeting him on the train and did everything she could to avoid it. But since he lived in Noroton Heights, it was sometimes unavoidable. Like today.

"Hello, Saul," she said absently.

"Is everything okay?" he asked, breathing deeply. "I've been calling you since Forty-Third Street."

"Yes, fine," she replied, beginning to move toward the platform entrance. "Just thinking about some work I have to do on the train." There was no reason she couldn't plant that seed in his mind now so he wouldn't be too hurt when she took a single seat. In truth she didn't want to do anything more strenuous than read the latest Michener book.

"There's plenty of time before the train comes," Bechner said, unable to keep the uncertain eagerness out of his voice. "Can I spell you with a cup of coffee?"

"Thanks for asking, Saul," she said, continuing to move toward the entrance, "but I'm really not in the mood." Time was when she'd make some sort of inaccurate excuse like "coffee makes me nervous," but she had learned that honesty was the best policy and, besides, he could take her "mood" any way he wanted.

"All right." He took it in stride. "I might as well wait for the train with you, then."

Alice turned away, rolling her eyes toward the ceiling when her back was to him. Together they walked down the ramp and took up position on the platform where the train's second "no smoking" car would be when it eased itself into the station.

Several other business people and visitors were congregating on the platform, but they were dwarfed by the massive labyrinth of tracks, concrete supports, metal cat-walks, and steaming trains resting in the bowels of Grand Central Station. It was a massive, nearly amazing maze of almost outdated technology barely kept in operation by a ridiculously complex system of tired men and dying machines.

Alice let her thoughts drift across Grand Central's outmoded industry straining to keep up with the commuters, rather than listening to Bechner's tired attempts at conversation. She would rather ponder the astonishing number of trains coming and going from all points to and from this gigantic building with its stench-ridden tunnels and rotting tracks.

It wasn't until she caught a snatch of Bechner's subject matter that she turned her attention to him. She heard something about what the rest of the office thought about her.

"I beg your pardon?" she asked.

The man was taken aback somewhat. When her head had been turned, he had felt more at ease. With her grey eyes focused on him, he felt guilty somehow. He looked at her perfectly made-up face with her perfectly done short, dark brown hair and felt foolish.

"I was saying that some men at the office were calling you the 'Ice Princess,'" Saul said quietly. "Until I set them straight."

"Oh?" she replied sharply. "And just how did you set them straight?"

Bechner was really flustered now. "It's just that..." he started. "Well, that's nothing to call a fellow executive," he recovered. "I said you have to be tough with the competition, but that is no reflection on your standing as a wo... person." He found himself backing up under her even, seemingly emotionless gaze.

He stopped only when he felt his leg brush against a garbage can. Grand Central had no time for finesse. Instead of a fanciful refuse container, there were large oil drums placed on the platforms. As usual they were brimming over with garbage.

Bechner stood his ground beside it. "They . . . they seemed to respect that," he finished.

Alice Lieberman stared at the man for a moment. She looked down the track as the 5:09 began edging its way down the track next to their platform. She saw she had enough time to make things clear to the sad case, so she left her briefcase to save her spot as more riders started appearing, then carefully approached Bechner.

"I appreciate your speaking up for me," she told him quietly. "But let's get one thing straight. My best . . . my only defense is my work. I don't care what anyone says about me, as long as they leave my work out of it. My work is the best. You know it, I know it, and they know it. And that's all anyone needs to know.

"So the next time you hear anything, just let them talk, all right? Don't even tell me. I don't want to know. I have too many important things on my mind." Without waiting for a reply, she returned to her position near the edge of the platform.

Saul Bechner could sense that his face was beet red. Thankfully the gloom of the tracks illuminated only by naked light bulbs was enough to hide that fact from the other passengers. He felt unbelievably stupid. He could take solace only in the fact that the approaching train had drowned out Lieberman's words from anyone else's ears. But he knew she would never look at him with respect now.

"Alice," he called, in spite of himself.

She turned toward him.

His mouth opened, but before any words could come out, the garbage can behind Bechner exploded.

To her, it looked positively cosmic. She heard him call her name. She looked at him. He was leaning slightly forward, one hand on the garbage can rim. Then a huge flash of red and yellow blossomed all around him. He

27

rose off the floor as flaming hunks of refuse and spinning shards of metal shot and spun out in all directions.

He flew toward her, like Superman, his mouth still open and his arms outstretched. As he came, the edges of his body were perforated, tattered, and torn off like confetti. He became his own cloud, which trailed him as he went. It was as if he were floating in an acid cloud that ate away at him as he went.

It seemed like many moments, but it was actually less than a second before Bechner's corpse flew across the platform and slammed into Alice. She was knocked off her feet and onto the tracks. She might have been lucky. After all, the brunt of the explosion was taken by Bechner and, once on the sunken tracks, the schrapnel and debris sliced the air above her.

But the train couldn't stop in time. She fell across the tracks right in front of the massive Conrail engine. Her legs went first—sliced, then broken off at midcalf. Then the metal guillotine-like wheels supporting the hundreds of tons of machinery ground into her face.

Chapter Three

No one deserves to die like that. Not Tamara Anderson, not Alice Lieberman, and especially not Barbara Oshikata.

She practically waltzed out of the bathroom, holding up the hemline of her new dress and twirling into the living room like a ballerina. Her young face was infused with happiness and anticipated pleasure. Her mother's face lit up like the star at the top of a Christmas tree, and even her father couldn't help but smile a little at the beautiful girl who danced before him.

But it was that very precious beauty that straightened his lips. "Are you going to wear that?" he said in dour disbelief.

His wife's head snapped in his direction as if radio-controlled. "Alex . . ." she warned.

Their daughter guilelessly took it the wrong way. "What's the matter with it?" she asked, cutting off her turns. "Is there something wrong?"

"No, of course not," her mother maintained, coming from around the open-air kitchen counter. "It's lovely, and you look absolutely perfect." She put her hands on her daughter's shoulders and looked at her with pride. But the girl was not fooled.

"Dad . . ."

The father looked up from the Oriental rugs on the

teakwood floor to his daughter's hopeful face. "I don't know what you expect from me," he said flatly. "You know how I feel about this."

"Alex." This time his wife's voice was filled with disappointment.

"I've made my feelings clear, Denise," he told her, standing. "You know this is very hard for me to accept."

"But *I* don't know that, Dad," Barbara Oshikata replied, suddenly serious. She came over to him. "You've never made your feelings clear to me."

He looked at her with great sadness. "I didn't think I'd have to." He walked around her and headed for his study. His daughter stopped him in the doorway.

"Don't shut me out," she pleaded. "I'm sorry if I failed you, Dad, but please, please tell me what I've done wrong."

Her voice was not totally plaintive. Beneath that surface emotion was a strong undercurrent of demand. She was trying to force him to face it himself. She knew as long as he kept avoiding the issue, it would never be resolved. He looked at her handsome face and the firm young body beneath her opal green dress, and he knew he had helped give birth to an extraordinary person.

He put his hand over hers on his shoulder. "You will make an exceptional scholar," he told her softly.

"That's next year," she said, her voice lightening. "Tonight I just want to go out knowing I have your blessing."

"You will always have my blessing." He stressed the word you.

Barbara strove to understand the hatred, the deep-seated bigotry that prevented her father from treating her boyfriend like a human being. "Don wasn't born in China, Dad," she attempted.

"His parents were," he said, turning away. "I'm sorry. I'm really sorry. Our country fought them too long. I cannot accept it. I cannot." He pushed his daughter's hands away and moved into the study. "Please, go with my blessings," she heard as he closed the door. "But be careful."

"Don won't let anything happen to me," she told the closed door. She bit her lip, turned back toward her mother and shrugged.

Denise Oshikata relaxed and came forward to hug her child. "It'll be all right," she promised. "At the end of the summer you'll go to college, and he'll forget all about it."

Barbara returned her mother's hug and then looked at her with a tired grin. "Will this happen every time I date a non-Japanese?"

"It's just the Chinese, dear," the woman said uncomfortably.

"He should've thought of that before getting a co-op so close to Chinatown," Barbara replied, breaking the clinch. She looked out the second-floor window onto West Broadway. To her left was the World Trade Center. To her right was the Empire State Building. They gleamed in the late summer night like monuments to humanity's achievements—or at least to construction workers'.

She turned back when she heard the front door buzzer. She beat her mother to the speaker at a flat out gallop. "Who is it?" she almost sang.

"Don," was the static-filled reply. No matter how modern these intercom devices, Barbara had yet to hear one that didn't sound as if the visitor was reporting from outer space.

"I'll be right down," she called. She went over to the couch and scooped up her purse.

"You be careful," her mother advised.

"I will," Barbara said on the way to the door. "Don't worry. And you'll videotape tonight's episode of *Sword of Vengeance,* right?"

"Is that the one with the baby cart?" Denise asked.

31

"Right, on cable channel J. Okay?"

"So right," Denise said with an exaggerated geisha accent while bowing. "Have a nice time. Don't stay out too late."

"Yes, Mother," Barbara replied with feigned exasperation. "No, Mother. You bet, Mother." Both women laughed.

"Get going, or your date will leave," the mother said.

"No chance," the daughter answered, and was gone.

Neither parent ever saw their little girl again.

Their eighteen-year-old little girl accompanied her eighteen-year-old date to a club he knew on the other side of the Pogoda Theater in Chinatown. They had a good dinner and a fine talk about what they were hoping to do in college that coming September. Barbara was going to Boston University, where a solid Oriental community was nestled just across the river at MIT. Don was all set to take Indiana State by storm, intent on getting his Master's in Business Administration.

Dad didn't have much reason to worry after all, Barbara decided. She doubted her affection would remain strong once they were separated by that distance.

When Don suggested a little serious extracurricular activity at his place, Barbara deflected his approach with a little dancing. If she had decided to lose her virginity, she would have saved both their lives. But the Oshikatas had raised a good girl.

That was no help when the three men entered and sprayed the club with bullets.

Barbara and Don were near the back wall when the lead smashed down the diners closest to the front door. Barbara's vision was blocked by a sudden surge of panicked patrons, but Don immediately dragged her to the floor.

"Stay down," he told her through clenched teeth, pulling most of his body across hers. For a split second she thought it was the most obvious approach she had ever

32

experienced, but then she realized Don couldn't have possibly arranged all this.

From her prone position she couldn't see anything clearly. She just got the impression of flailing bodies, acrid smoke, and shattering dishes. A sudden jolt came when someone stepped on them in blind panic to get away. The foot landed half on Don and half on her. She had just gotten over that shock when the same person fell heavily back, smashing his head on the floor right in front of her face.

All she could see was his greasy, unkempt black hair. She tried to slide backwards, but Don held her tightly in place. "No," he warned. "Keep still."

The sharp cracking noises began to lessen, the sound of breaking dishes began to diminish, and the frenzied movement began to slow. Barbara could feel the weight across her back begin to lessen, but heard the distant crashing of fighting from outside.

She dared sitting up, only to find Don staring beyond the front doors as if he were a retriever on a hunting trip. All at once the rest of the restaurant patrons decided to leave. They charged the front doors en masse, just in time to catch a molotov cocktail.

The glass shattered in a shower of flame as the liquid caught fire amid the spinning shards. The dark club interior was etched in bright light as the clamoring diners were thrown into silhouette. Suddenly the two seemed to mix, and the people were covered in waves of fire.

They came screaming back as Don grabbed the girl and pulled her toward the kitchen. He stopped only for a second, and that was to shout at some people trying to fight their way into the bathrooms.

"No! That's the second place . . . !"

The lavs were suddenly dripping with flames as well, dousing the occupants with burning liquid. Mercifully the john doors closed before Barbara saw any more.

The quiet club had changed into an inferno. For a

second Barbara saw it as a huge oven filled with the dead and dying her father must have witnessed at the end of World War II.

She could suddenly understand his feelings, the bigotry he couldn't shake. She could understand his unreasoning hatred for anything that added to the pain of those final days. And she felt the horror of being unable to tell him so.

Don shielded her with his body as they pushed through the swinging doors into the kitchen. The cooks and helpers were all trying to squeeze through one tiny door on the far side. Barbara watched as they were thrown back by another burst of liquid flame. It was an explosion of fire that made a crackling, deadly hot wall between them and the outside.

Don pushed her against the sink and shoved the dishwashing sprayer into her hand. He turned both faucets all the way on. "Use this to keep the flames away!" he shouted above the roar of the flames. "I'll get you out of here, I swear!"

He tried to move away, but Barbara clamped one hand onto his jacket. "What is it?" she gasped.

"Tong!" he yelled. "It's a gang war! They shoot their enemy, then burn their headquarters!"

Barbara still wouldn't let go. "How . . . how do you know? Are you . . . ?"

"Used to be!" he swore, pulling off his jacket. "I'll get out! I'll save you! Just use the water, all right?"

He turned and grabbed two potholders. Then he pulled up a large baking pan that could cover him from the waist up. He knocked the burning men aside and charged right into the flame wall. It swept outwards, like doors to a Western saloon, then snapped back shut behind him.

Barbara stood, her knees weak, one hand on the hot sink to keep her upright. In the other hand was the sprayer, which was attached to the sink by a spring-covered rubber pipe. She stared at the opening where Don had disap-

34

peared, her mind unable to fully grasp what was happening to her. She was suddenly brought back to reality when a flame got too close to her.

With a start, she felt the pain and swung the hose in that direction. By pressing the tab, she shot a powerful stream of water. It quelled the encroaching flame with an angry hiss. Barbara became aware that she was almost entirely surrounded by flame. She saw water pipes above her, but the safety nozzles—installed for this very emergency—failed to turn on.

She heard a popping sound that brought her eyes back to the kitchen doorway. Something dark was rising out of the flames there. It continued to grow as she watched, until it took on the unmistakeable form of a head. The body followed, blackened and charred by the heat. But there were three unmistakeable bullet holes in the torso.

The human shaped thing lumbered forward like Frankenstein's monster, its baked skin flaking off it. The shriveled lips opened and mouthed her name. Then it fell forward. Don had lied. He would not save her.

Barbara dropped the water hose and ran blindly back into the dining room. She had entered Hell from the frying pan, into the fire. Almost everyone who wasn't dead was writhing on the ground. The flames had spread throughout the restaurant. Rancid black smoke was boiling across the high ceiling. The girl could scarcely see or breathe.

Coughing, dizzy, she stumbled back to the booth where she had been sitting, her memory shrieking at her. As she fell on the smoldering sofa seats, she remembered seeing the emergency fire hose behind its glass door three booths down. She pulled herself up and forced herself in that direction. She had got only five steps when she tripped.

Barbara fell over a slowly frying corpse with most of its jaw smashed away by a bullet. What flesh was left was bubbling from the heat. The girl looked away, but this

35

gruesome vision reminded her of the "Learn Not to Burn" commercials on television. She remembered its warning to keep close to the ground in a fire.

She crawled forward, most of her body numb, as if she had fallen asleep at the beach in the noonday sun. She ignored all the sensations and just concentrated on getting to the fire hose. She rounded the last booth and was greeted by a burning bush. A potted plant beneath the hose had caught fire. She shoved it out of the way and pulled herself upright.

Her hand was nearly seared to the metal door when she gripped the handle. She wrenched her arm back, her nerves screaming in pain. She fell back against the booth, her vision blinded by tears. A second later she had planted both feet and was up again, her agony replaced by anger. Enraged, she grabbed a plate off the nearest table and smashed it into the glass.

The shards stabbed into her arm, but she continued to ignore it. She pushed her good hand through the opening and pulled the hose out. It's canvas covering and metal tip smashed the rest of the pane aside. Pushing it under her wounded arm, she reached for the water wheel. With incredible effort she turned it around, her lips widening in a wolf-like smile.

Any second she expected to feel the surge of water. Any second she expected to clear a path to reach the front door. Any second she expected to dispel the pain and frustration clouding her mind.

Nothing happened. She dropped the hose and wrenched the wheel around with both hands. It opened all the way, but nothing happened. The hose was dry.

Barbara Oshikata fell back against the wall, sobbing. She slid down to the floor, all the pain, all the horror finally reaching her. Her eyes vacantly took in the thickening cloud of smoke and the widening trail of fire until her vision was filled with yellow and black.

In the distance there was a stab of red. She saw it—

first dimly, and then clearly among the rolling smoke. It was four letters hovering in the air. It was four letters required by law—E-X-I-T.

It was like a leash that pulled at Barbara's throat, choking her. Her legs and arms were already moving before she was even aware of them. She was half crawling, half jumping across the smoldering carpet. She felt the nylons on her legs beginning to melt. She felt her beautiful opal dress beginning to ignite. She felt her eyebrows and lashes crumble into ash. She even felt her blood begin to boil.

But she reached the door. She reached the door, and she reached up to the automatic panel that would open it with a push. She slammed her hand against it. It wouldn't budge.

She heard an animal-like noise tearing out of her throat. It gave her the strength to get up. She threw her entire weight against the panel. It gave way.

But the door wouldn't open.

She heard the alarm go off. She was dimly aware of the light that went on over the obstruction. The emergency panel was working, but the door was locked from the other side.

On the other side an implacable padlock held the emergency exit door fast. On the other side of the thick door could be heard the noise of Barbara's fists pounding against the partition.

The first of those who ran down to the street from neighboring buildings heard the sound, but they could do nothing about it. After a while only the dimmest of scratching could be heard.

Then nothing.

No, no one deserves to die like that. Not Tamara Anderson, not Alice Lieberman, and not Barbara Oshikata. Especially not Barbara Oshikata. Her death was not like the others. Tamara had lost consciousness on the third hit. Alice had been knocked unconscious by the fall. But Barbara had remained aware to the last second. She did not know whether she had died from the flames or suffocation.

No, no one deserves to die like that. Not when the police saw their deaths as three unrelated fatalities. Not when the many others who had died with them were written off as unfortunate victims of the "Manhattan malaise," the illness that saw more than two dozen people murdered on a good day in New York City.

No, no one deserves to die like that. Except for the people who killed them.

Chapter Four

Baby Blue was closest to the door, so Baby Blue was the first to die.

The door was awkwardly stuck into a wall that seemed to turn at that juncture. It was made to swing in, just barely leading to a shoe-box shaped living area where Johnny Stick crammed in his kitchen table, the sink, two beds, a dresser drawer, and a bathtub.

The table was under the small window leading to the air shaft outside and the sink was next to the same window. One bed was between the sink and the dresser. Both beds were parallel to each other, separated by a distance of two feet, and both lay at the base of two barred windows.

The bathtub was at the base of the second bed. It was filled with water, which was in turn filled with Connie C., Johnny Stick's latest squeeze. The Blond couldn't take his blue eyes off the girl as she sat naked under the milky white city water. He sat just behind Johnny while Bob One, Bob Two, and Bilgrey sat around the rest of the table.

Johnny had something about the letter B. That's why all his boys were nicknamed that way and that's why his gang was called the Killer B's.

Nobody was in the adjoining room behind the door,

which was littered with pieces of furniture. There were no windows in there, so there was no light. About the only thing in there was a thick heating pipe that rose from floor to ceiling.

"It's fucking August," said Baby Blue, "and the fucking super hasn't turned off the fucking heat yet." The windows were open, so no one else complained. Only the Baby, because that was the way he was. And he was closest to the door, so he was the first to die when the man came through the door.

The man didn't just knock the obstruction aside; he came through the damn thing, smashing the panels open while ripping the top hinge out of the wall. They was no warning to the attack. One minute the guys were talking. The next, a bald, bull-headed man had plowed through the doorway of the eighth-floor apartment.

Baby Blue was thrown forward by the debris, keeping just in front of the charging man. He moored himself in the entrance to the living room, thinking he could lash back at his attacker. His body stopped and his arm swung, but the man kept coming.

He ducked under Blue's arm and wrapped one of his own around the kid's torso. He ran into the room, throwing the kid right into the air. Blue was getting his air legs just as he landed on the rusty fold-out kitchen table. It held his weight and acted like a tightly strung trampoline.

Blue dived shoulder first into the wall as everything on the table jumped up. The metal tube legs slipped out from under, and the piece of furniture dumped its remaining contents on Bob One, the Blond, and Bob Two. Blue slid down the wall and slammed into the sink.

The Baby may have been a complainer, but he was a great in-fighter. That's why Johnny kept him around. Just when everyone else was getting used to the idea of a mad human bull in their midst, Blue was vaulting out of the sink, in a screaming dive.

The mad bull met him straight on. As the others

40

watched in amazement, the man's massive arms swung, catching Blue in his side in midair. There was a powerful thud, and then the Baby was writhing in the sky toward the air-shaft window. He clawed at the wall, screeching, as the man's blow pushed him through the opening.

The force of his momentum was too much for his skinny fingers. The weak plastered walls were left with some shallow grooves, but Blue seemed to be sucked right out of the window, like the villain at the end of *Goldfinger*. The rest heard the very beginning of his scream as he fell the seven stories, but were then too busy to listen anymore.

Bilgrey, once known by his parents as William Grey, immediately dove for the dresser. He grabbed the sawed-off two by four laying against its far side. They didn't call the leader Johnny Stick for nothing. Bilgrey had grabbed his weapon. It was a board with two nails coming out of every side at its crown, including the top.

Bilgrey swung it as the man came in close. The mad bull blocked the board with his forearm, the nails just touching the surface of his black T-shirt. The man's right foot lashed out, smashing into Bilgrey's groin. The gang member literally slid back on both feet from the force of the blow, his testicles and penis completely crushed.

He fell back across the first bed, close to death, as the mad bull whirled, the stick now in his hand. His sudden turn sent the handle of the club across the Blond's jaw. He had tried to jump the man from behind, but spun hard into the wall and slid to the floor.

The force of the blow kept the stick swinging. The man let it swing all the way around until he caught the handle in midair. Johnny didn't notice any of this. He was too busy digging in the pocket of his jacket, which was hung on a nail above the tub. Connie was shrieking beneath him, trying to push him out of her way.

Johnny pulled the "Saturday Night Special" gun free of the jacket cloth and swung toward the bull just as he swung the club. Two nails dug into Johnny's wrist and palm, pushing his arm back the way it had come, ripping open the flesh as it went. The gun flew out of his hand, bounced off the overturned table edge and clattered into the corner.

Johnny took a step back, pulling his hand free of the club. Ignoring the wound, he leaped forward just as the man let the club blow swing him around. Johnny was sure he could smash into the guy while his back was turned. Incredibly the man seemed to snake inside out.

Normally a savage roundhouse blow with a club like that would throw someone off balance and expose his back to the other fighter. Johnny was taking advantage of that when the man twisted his club-holding wrist downwards, let go of the stick so it swung down, grabbed it again when the nails were pointing in the other direction, and stabbed backwards.

The nail end of the club came right at Johnny from the man's back. The top nails bit him in the chest as the man pivoted on his toes so he was facing forward again, his club arm twisted back. The bull pushed, plucking Johnny up off his feet and sending him crashing into the tub back first.

Connie howled as the gang leader's body smashed onto her legs. The water flew in all directions, half-emptying the tub. But half the water was enough to hold Johnny's head under the surface. The girl fell forward, clawing at the man's face. His free hand shot out, the flat of his palm catching her under the jaw.

There was a snap, and Connie's naked body jumped backwards, as if she were in the Olympic diving trials. She landed on her neck and shoulders, somersaulting backwards. Johnny was clawing at the club, trying to slip out from under the water and the nail tips.

The bull-like attacker looked over to see the two Bobs scrambling for their gun. With a sudden shove he pushed the nails into Johnny's chest up to their heads. The gang leader jerked once, then lay still beneath the bath water. The man pulled the stick out just as Bob Two brought up the revolver.

The man screamed, then ducked behind the tub when Bob Two pulled the trigger. A shattering sound filled the room as the gunpowder exploded and the bullet took a hunk out of the tub top. Bob Two was about to shoot again but stopped when the tub unbelievably started to be lifted.

The base rose and then tipped toward the two Bobs. Bob Two fired twice more, ripping holes in their dead leader and the bath bottom. The water and Johnny came tumbling out just before there was a wrenching noise and the tub came free of its pipe moorings.

The metal bath tumbled forward as the broken pipes began spraying out water. The man charged from out of the spray, holding the tub up as a shield. Bob Two managed to get off one more shot before the tub slammed into him.

It was a Bob Two sandwich, human meat slapped between the tub and wall. The force of the blow broke most of his teeth as well as his nose. Bob One slid out of the room just as his comrade's blood began to spurt out of his broken face. Bob One was almost out of the apartment when the nails of Johnny's stick slammed into the door frame.

He fell back into the adjoining room. Shouting in terror, he threw everything he could get his hands on at the approaching killer. The man simply swatted it aside with the club, like slow pitches thrown at Hank Aaron. Only this man wasn't black. The light from the other room showed the man's face clearly. It showed the bald, gleaming head. It showed the yellowish skin. It showed the almond-shaped eyes.

Bob One grabbed the last piece of furniture in both

43

hands and hurled it with all his might. The Oriental attacker finally planted his feet, stood his ground, and swung the club with all his might.

The bat cracked against the heavy sofa, but managed to knock it aside. Bob One didn't see the club break and in two pieces. He was pulling up his pant leg whipping out his switchblade. He got it up and open before he saw the broken stick. He smiled, thinking he was finally one up on the attacker.

"Come on, man," he goaded, slowly moving the blade from side to side. "I'm ready for you now."

The man looked at the bat, looked at the grinning tough, and then threw the stick handle down. Bob One winced at the cracking sound when the handle brutally hit the floor, but he didn't lose his composure completely.

"Where'd you come from, man?" he drawled. "Who sent you, huh? The Tiger Claws? Who?"

The man said nothing; just slowly walked across the floor, his head down in shadow.

"What do you want from us, man?" Bob One said more stridently. "We didn't do nothing! We ain't been in Chinatown, man, I swear it!" He wasn't used to facing the gang's enemy alone.

The man just kept walking. Bob One kept backing away until his back was against the far wall. He held his knife out, but that didn't deter the man at all. Finally the attacker stopped three feet away from the first Bob.

"Hey, you want to talk?" the kid almost babbled in relief. "Great, man, that's just great. Hey, I don't know what the problem is, but if Johnny overstepped the line, I can dig it. He deserved whatever he got, you know?"

The man wasn't listening. He was moving his arms rhythmically while breathing deeply in a crouched position. Bob One had seen enough Bruce Lee films to know what was going on. The guy was about to lay into him with some kung fu.

Normally Bob One would have laughed it off. But he

44

had seen in the other room what this guy could do, and he had seen what Bruce Lee, Bruce Li, Bruce Le, and Bruce Liang could do in movies and on TV, so his knife hand began to get a little shaky.

Just as he was working up to charging the man, he saw the Blond appear from over the bull's left shoulder. He practically fainted in relief. Together they could make quick work of the bastard. The Blond had his own knife out and was quickly moving forward in silence. Bob One stabbed forward with his knife just as the Blond's blade seemed destined to sink into the man's back.

It was like right out of the martial arts movies. The man's leg shot back, streaking right by the knife, his foot smashing into the Blond's face. At the same time, his left arm swung forward, deflecting Bob One's blow. As soon as his leg came back, his right fist flashed forward, crushing Bob One's nose.

The Blond fell heavily on the floor, propped up by the far wall. Bob One's head snapped back and slammed into the heating pipe. Before he could fall forward, the man screamed in a kung fu yell, spun around and let the side of his foot nearly take off the kid's face.

Bob One followed his teeth to the side wall where his head slammed into the plaster. The knife stayed in his hand as his body shivered, held upright since his skull was three inches deep into the wall. The man stared at his handiwork along with the Blond. But while the remaining gang member's face was horrified, the killer's face was placid.

The Blond scrambled across the wall and half dove, half crawled for the door. He fell out into the hallway, bellowing for help. The three other doors on the floor remained tightly shut. The Blond instinctively knew they would not open for him. The Killer's B's had done too much to the place's residents. He should have been surprised they weren't selling tickets to the gang's dismemberment.

He moved forward on hands and knees until he found his feet. As they slammed on the rotting floorboards heading toward the stairs, he heard them echoing. The killer was right behind him.

Adrenaline flooded through the Blond's veins, practically shooting him onto the stairs. As he rounded the banister to go down the first flight, he felt more than heard a figure vaulting over the railing. The killer landed in front of him. Without waiting the Oriental chopped the blade from the Blond's hand and sliced his fingers into his throat.

Binding pain lanced up into the Blond's brain. A yellow-orange sheet covered his head as he felt himself being lifted up. He could see nothing and feel nothing. There was a roaring sound in his ears as he felt himself floating upwards.

Suddenly the pressure was gone. With it went the veil of pain and the crashing noise. The first thing he saw was the city. It was a glorious, twinkling gem spread out in all directions from the roof of the decrepit Houston Street brownstone. The Blond stumbled toward the ledge before a settling hand gripped him on the back of the neck.

"Tell me about the Tiger Claws," said a hoarse, guttural voice.

Chapter Five

It was sunk on the inside pages in the second section of the *New York Times*. It was a minor story halfway into the ten o'clock news telecast. It was the third lead-in on *Live at Five*. It was the red-banner headline in the *New York Post*: SIX TOUGHS SLAUGHTERED! The large black subheading read MASSACRE IN SOHO.

All the reports said the same thing. A street gang known as the Killer B's were found murdered in their apartment house headquarters the other day, all apparent victims of a gang war presently being waged citywide.

The other occupants of the rundown building on West Houston Street saw and heard nothing. The police admit to having no clues or leads to exactly who or exactly which rival gang led the attack, but available evidence on the scene seems to indicate that it was the work of at least a half-dozen other youths.

The police report added some extra details. A gun was found on the premises, as were several knives, a club, and some drug paraphernalia. The whole apartment looked like a hurricane had hit it.

Jonathan Dunne had a stab wound in the heart. Robert Williams died of a concussion. Robert Glynn and William Grey died of shock. Gilbert Farley took a seven-story fall. Matt Kelley, also known as the Blond, took an eight-story drop. He was found half on the sidewalk, half in the street in front of the building.

Alex and Denise Oshikata saw none of these reports. He was still cloistered in his den, the lights out. She was sitting in the living room, staring blindly at the television. It was playing the same thing over and over again. It was Saturday's episode of *Sword of Vengeance*. Whenever it would end, Denise Oshikata would rise from the sofa like a zombie, rewind the video, and start it again.

Their guest watched it two times with her. Occasionally he would try to start a conversation. She reacted to it the same way she reacted to the show's dialogue—as if she hadn't heard it at all. She had been watching it when he had first appeared at their door. They wouldn't answer the buzzer, so he had waited until the reporters left, then picked the lock. Now the bald, muscular Oriental got up from the easy chair as *Sword of Vengeance*'s hero, the disgraced *Shogun*'s executioner Itto Ogami, ran through a hut, chopping down his enemies as they thrust spears at him through the straw walls. He walked between Denise and the set, but she didn't seem to notice. He knocked on the study door.

He kept knocking until Alex was forced to answer. When he heard who it was, the grieving father unlocked the door. Denise was watching the show even then. Alex explained why. He told him that she would keep watching until she fell asleep. Whenever he switched off the set, she would awake screeching. Nothing would placate her but the videotape-recorded episode.

Alex hadn't seemed to recognize him when he opened it. Behind him the room was still dark, and it took some seconds before his eyes adjusted. Finally his vision cleared, and he smiled at his brother. "Hama," he said with comfort.

"I am going now," said the once affable, once stocky cook for the Rhea Dawn restaurant in Sausalito. He no longer looked like the cheerful Buddha—always in the

48

white karate pants and sleeveless T-shirt. He wore a tan overcoat now, with dark pants and plain shoes beneath its calf-length hem.

"Will you return?" Oshikata asked.

Hama paused before answering. "I don't know," he said honestly.

Oshikata bowed slightly. "Thank you for sharing in our grief," he said automatically.

Hama quickly, irritably straightened Alex up by grabbing his bent shoulders. "The time for grief has ended," he said firmly. "It is time for retribution."

Oshikata's eyes looked right through Hama. "Against who? For what? We killed Barbara."

"Don't talk like that," Hama snapped. "Someone murdered her. I'm going to find out who."

"We killed her," the man maintained hollowly. "This city killed her."

"No one believes that," Hama said with certainty, trying to make his words drill through his brother's thick skull. "You cannot blame yourself for the act of a murderer. The only way is to make the killer pay."

Alex Oshikata did not reply to that. His mind was gripped with thoughts of guilt. Guilt that he allowed his daughter out that night against his better judgment. Guilt that he allowed his wife to convince him. Guilt that he brought his loved ones to such a hateful place.

"I'm going now," Hama repeated quietly. He looked back at Denise before returning his strong gaze to the man. "You should too," he told him meaningfully.

"But . . . ," Oshikata stammered. "We cannot. Denise . . ."

"Take her out of here," Hama instructed. "Let her scream for a while. Let her cry. It is the only means to wash the memories away."

"We cannot," Alex said firmly. "We haven't buried her yet. The police . . ." His steady voice began to falter. "The police have not . . . completely identified her yet. They

49

can't . . . can't tell . . . which one . . . is . . ." Oshikata quickly closed the door in Hama's face.

The disgrace and shame was too much for him to bear. His only child dead in a Chinese gang war—burned so badly with so many others that the authorities were unable to identify the remains until a thorough dental examination of each charred skull was made.

Hama's resolve was doubled. He pulled the thin tan overcoat more securely around himself and walked out of the apartment, down the stairs, and out into the hot night air. As usual the streets were alight with activity. Soho was crammed full of bistros, galleries, and eccentric shops. Directly to the west was Little Italy, its narrow streets awash with strung light bulbs, pasta houses, and cappucino bars.

Further north this Italian section smacked head-on with Chinatown. On several streets, like Mulberry, one ended and the other started seemingly in mid-building, as if someone had drawn a distinct boundary line and both races snuggled right up against it, neither stepping over.

But once someone stepped on Canal Street, it was Chinese territory. Bracketed by the police station and the courts on the north side, Soho on the east, Little Italy on the south, and the bridge to Brooklyn on the west, Chinatown was filled with residents and tourists selling, buying, and eating.

Hama walked from Oshikata's West Broadway co-op to the corner of Canal Street and Bowery. Directly in front of him was the L'Arc de Triumphe-like arch that marked the bridge entrance. To his right was Confucious Square. To his left were two movie theaters.

The Chinatown Theater was playing the latest release from Seasonal Films, the Hong Kong-based company that gave Jackie Chan his big break. Since that martial arts superstar went independent, their latest hero's name was translated into English as "Conan Lee." Ironically his first film was titled *Ninja in the Dragon's Den*.

Hama looked further down the street to The Music Palace. It was exclusively a Shaw Brothers theater, showing only the ample output of that major Chinese producer. Today they were featuring the latest film by Liu Chia-liang, the best martial arts director working.

As much as Hama wished he could just see the movies and then go home to a happy Oshikata family, he knew it couldn't be. He turned away from the theaters and walked across the street to Confucious Square. The square was made by a gigantic apartment house that was bordered on one side by a high school.

All of this was in the shadow of the massive bridge, held aloft by gigantic fenced-in supports. It was an awesome structure with only one building nestled directly under it. That was the Sun Sung Cinema, an independentally owned theater that showed Golden Harvest Studio films as well as the cheaper independent Hong Kong movie product.

There was nothing on either side of it and nothing across the street except one massive bridge support. There wasn't much traffic along the road either. Hama came late during the second showing, correctly assuming that not many prospective viewers would be hanging around the dark lobby. Before going in he pulled a crumpled hat out of his pocket. It folded out to cover his head while its downward brim shielded his eyes.

He entered the building to look down the long, sloping entry hall, lined with posters and pictures of upcoming films. There were action, romances, costume dramas, and martial arts efforts soon to be shown. Nestled in the far left corner of the lobby was the box office and snack bar, which were both closed.

Hama walked up to the six closed doors to the theater, slipped the far right one open, and moved directly to the

51

nearby balcony stairway. He automatically went up the steps, his eyes adjusting to the gloom while his ears picked up the singsong incantations of Cantonese.

When he reached the balcony proper, he could see the two sections of six rows each almost completely filled. Above and beyond that was the main floor, a large stage, and the big screen upon which a Chinese girl was pleading with her warrior husband not to do battle. The words fell on deaf ears in the film and on Hama as well.

He saw the monogrammed jackets of the Tiger Claws as he moved purposefully for the front six rows. He was about to step on the first stair in that section when a waiting teen came up from the side, his hand gripping Hama's upper arm.

"Old man," the T-shirted tough said quietly in Mandarin, "no seats here. You go downstairs, okay?"

Hama instantly took on a cowed, agreeable persona, ducking low and nodding his head as if he were a toothless codger. He stepped back to see the tough take up his previous position on a chair in front of the emergency-exit double door. He was a guard, placed to make sure no one bothered the other Tiger Claws while they enjoyed the film. No doubt there was another just like him on the other side.

Hama moved cautiously to the stairway, walked down it slowly, and left the theater. Looking both ways down the street, he moved along the side wall of the building until he came to the exit stairway. It was a set of thin metal steps. Hama moved silently up them until he reached the steel slat landing.

He placed one palm against the crack where the two doors met. He could feel the Tiger Claw guard's aura heat from the other side. Making sure his body blocked any innocent bystander from witnessing, Hama opened his coat and pulled out the short *waki-zashi* blade from the holster strapped to his upper leg.

It slipped out easily, gleaming darkly in the moonlight

52

filtering through the bridge beams. The handle was pitch black, giving Hama's eyes the impression that the blade alone was floating in midair. But he felt the solid weight and strength of the handle in his muscular hand.

Hama moved back, then thrust the thin, razor sharp blade through the crack and into the back of the resting guard.

The Tiger Claw started in surprise, his eyes wide as his mind acknowledged the strange sensation of steel cutting through his organs. The blade was sharp, and Hama's strike so strong, the guard was not pushed forward. By the time his body was ready to react, he was already dead. He slumped slightly when Hama pulled the sword out, but his eyes were still wide open and his body still sat. Hama slipped the blade quickly back into its scabbard and retraced his steps just as the film's fight scenes began in earnest.

All eyes were glued to the screen when Hama returned to the theater, moved silently up the balcony steps, walked right by the dead guard, and slipped casually into the aisle directly behind the person the Killer B Blond had marked as the gang leader. He had high cheek bones, wiry muscles, and black hair styled short in the front while long in the back. The rest of his gang called him Number One.

The other Tiger Claws complained as he moved by, but they thought nothing of it since their guards wouldn't let anyone who didn't belong through without causing a fuss. Besides, Number One often invited "business associates" to meet with him here. No one paid the plain little man in the raincoat and slouch hat any mind as he sat in the empty chair behind their leader.

Hama pulled the sword from its sheath as he sat. It pushed to the right and then to the left, slipping between his neighbor's ribs and into their hearts almost faster than the eye could see. They sighed and slumped. Without waiting Hama placed the tip against Number One's seat back and pushed forward.

At that exact second his girlfriend decided to turn for a little kiss. Although her eyes were centered on his neck, her peripheral vision couldn't help picking up the blade that was emerging from his chest.

Hama had timed it perfectly. As the fighters were screaming their attack yells on screen, the girl shrieked in horror. The sword disappeared from Number One's chest and Hama was already standing up and twisting. He brought the blade around above his head in a defensive hold, so it chopped into the neck of the Tiger Claw who was getting up behind him.

The blade coursed across the tough's throat, ripping open the veins and sending him writhing atop the gang member to his right. Hama stopped his swing in midflight and brought it back to the wounded kid's left. Since it was in the defensive position—the hilt at his pinky instead of his forefinger—he was able to thrust it deep into the other Tiger Claw's chest.

He immediately pulled it out and swung it to his left in order to chop down the frenzied tough who was pushing his way out from under the Tiger Claw with the hacked throat. He was wiping the other guy's blood out of his eyes when Hama's blade cut across his chest.

Hardly ten seconds had passed and already a half-dozen gang members were dead or dying. But there were a lot more, and they were becoming fully aware of what was going on. Hama ignored the others. He had eliminated all the immediate threats around him. He turned back toward the screen, stepped up on Number One's chair back, and leaped over the balcony banister.

Hama had already relegated the theater floor plan to memory. He knew how far and in which direction to jump in order to land in the aisle. He reached his first objective, rolled, and came up running for the exit at the right of the screen before anyone realized what was going on.

The door was padlocked—chained from the outside.

Hama whirled to see the rest of the Tiger Claws pouring down the stairs and vaulting off the balcony. Their hurtling bodies was enough to throw the rest of the audience in a panic. They charged in all directions, blocking the gang members from their quarry.

But unlike Hama, the Tiger Claws weren't averse to knocking off anyone who got in their way. Machetes, switchblades, bayonets, *sais, tonfas,* and *tokusho keibos* came out from under jackets and belts. They swung the American and Oriental weapons madly, smashing innocent people as they struggled toward their enemy.

Hama raced for the left exit on the other side of the screen. The Tiger Claws managed to get through to block him. Grabbing the *waki-zashi* hilt in both hands he moved to confront them. The first held a *sai*: a black-plated spike with a hilt that twisted parallel to the blade in an L shape. Martial arts masters use it to deflect swords and disarm attackers.

The first Tiger Claw was not an expert. He brought it forward as a stabbing weapon. Hama chopped across his forearm with the short samurai sword. The blow ripped open his skin and pushed the *sai* to the right, exposing the kid's torso. Hama kicked out to the side, sending the wounded tough back into the screen.

The first Tiger Claw fell to the ground as Hama sidled forward to meet the second tough head on. The Tiger Claw was swinging a *tokusho keibo*—a metal rod that could telescope out to four times its length at a push of a button. The guy thought he was being clever by going for Hama's sword first.

Hama twisted the blade out from under the swing, then thrust forward, the sword entering the kid's body from his armpit. Hama used the momentum to send both of them stumbling back to the other exit door. He slammed the struggling gang member against the opening rod. It was working, but this door too was chained from the outside.

Hama pivoted just as a third Tiger Claw swung down his machete. The second tough, still stuck on Hama's sword, became his shield and it was he who took the machete blade in the shoulder. He screamed in renewed pain, scrambling to pull himself off the *waki-zashi*.

Hama felt the blade scraping against the poor bastard's rib cage. He tried jerking it out, but it wouldn't come. What did come was a fifth gang member with a hardwood *tonfa*. This was a club with a handle, and the new attacker was swinging it down at Hama with all his might.

Hama pulled over the boy dying on the sword to serve as his shield again. Only, this time the Tiger Claw had no intention of coming. He held back, blood cascading out of his wounds. The *tonfa* smashed into the *waki-zashi* blade just as the wounded gang member fell.

The combination of the two attacks broke the blade. Hama fell backwards as the shielding boy dropped to the floor, a corpse. The shocked ninja-trained assassin slammed against the stage proscenium as the encircling gang members moved back to prevent being hit by their fallen associate.

The theater was silent, save for the movie soundtrack pumping out of the speakers behind the screen as the two adversaries summed up their positions. There were nine Tiger Claws left: all armed with deadly weapons. Hama stood with his back to the stage, a broken short samurai sword in both hands.

The gang moved in as Hama spun and leaped. He landed on his knees on the stage, blades plunking down just short of his feet. He pulled himself forward, heading for the screen. He tried to jump through the white material, but it was too strong and too tightly moored.

He knew he didn't have time to cut through with what was left of his blade. He slid down the screen to his feet and turned to face the Tiger Claws. They had moved in slowly, knowing he was trapped. All they had to see was

56

his yellow skin and slanted eyes to assume he had attacked them for some valid Oriental reason.

It could have been one of their many robberies. It could have been one of their many rapes. It could have been one of their many drug deals. It could have even been because of one of their many rumbles. Whatever the reason, he had killed some of their people, and they had him dead to rights.

Like the jungle beast they were named for, one gang member sped forward, a bayonet aimed straight at Hama's heart.

Chapter Six

The bayonet broke in midair.

The Tiger Claw gang member blinked and reared back. His blade hadn't merely dropped off; it had snapped with a sudden surge of downward power.

And he didn't just rear back. He was thrown back by the same force moving upward. He felt nothing after that, but his fellows saw his face fly off.

The Tiger Claw man's feet left the stage as he arced over backwards; his lips, nose, and brow flying in all directions. His features were replaced by crimson liquid.

The others watched in amazement—none more so than Hama's. They turned their heads to see their comrade fall behind them. Hama watched as hunks of four more Tiger Claw skulls flicked up into the air. The quartet—two on each side of the semicircle—reacted as if rabbit punched. Their heads rocked on their necks, and they collapsed.

The remaining four Tiger Claws whirled around trying to understand what had happened to their fallen friends. They and Hama saw the four-pointed *shuriken* sticking out of the heads at the same time. Then Hama felt himself being pulled back through the movie screen.

He emerged on the other side through a hair-thin slice in the screen. Even before he had regained his balance, the hat was pulled off his head and hands were taking the raincoat from his arms. It took him only a second to recognize his rescuers, then he was quickly abetting their switch of clothing.

Brett Wallace slipped into the tan overcoat without letting go of his *katana*. It was far stronger than Hama's broken *waki-zashi* since it was made by an Oriental craftsman in no less than six months. The hat was already covering his sandy hair, grey eyes and most of his other bland features. "Get him out of here," he instructed. "We'll meet later."

His instructions were not to be questioned. Rhea Tagashi and Jeff Archer moved on either side of Hama, but the cook could not quell his shame. "Sensei . . ." he began.

"Later," Brett said flatly. "Now these witnesses must die."

To the remaining Tiger Claws it seemed as if Hama had disappeared through the still solid screen. They had no way of knowing that Brett had sliced through the oncoming bayonet and then brought the blade back up across the attacking thug's face without making a tear in the material wider than a pinprick.

And they could not see the black *shurikens* as they sped from Jeff's and Rhea's hands into their comrades' skulls. Confused, angered, and frightened, they surged forward to investigate. Brett emerged from behind the screen at that second.

The theater had not completely emptied out. The last remaining patrons were pushing to escape at the very rear of the orchestra section. One man glanced back to see the final death of the Tiger Claw gang.

To this innocent eyewitness it looked as if the man in the tan coat and slouch hat was doing a dance somewhat between an Irish jig and roller disco. He weaved in and out of the remaining four fighters, his arms slashing in every direction. He moved right, sliced left, ducked down, spun, chopped down, faced forward, and fell to one knee.

60

All four Tiger Claws stood frozen in strange positions behind him. Incredibly the Cantonese characters for the words THE END flashed on the movie screen just as the man in the hat and raincoat stood. As he rose, the four others fell. The lights came on, and the curtain closed.

Without looking up the man in the raincoat hopped off the stage and walked out the left emergency exit. Only now it was no longer locked. The witness ran down the aisle as Tiger Claw blood pooled on the stage, then dribbled over the proscenium lip.

The witness gingerly avoided the puddles of blood on the floor and reached the exit. He swung open the door and looked out into the adjoining garbage-strewn lot. The man in the raincoat was not to be seen. Beyond the barren field was the sidewalk filled with escaped patrons. Beyond that was the roar of the bridge traffic above.

The witness blinked, shook his head, closed the door, and waited for the police to come. Did he have a story for them!

No one paid any attention to the man walking through Greenwich Village. There was no reason to heed the man of medium height wearing the dark slacks and light blue cotton shirt. With his plain features he blended in with the environment. He could have been an actor hoping for a job in commercials or a businessman relaxing after a tough day at the office.

In short, he could have been anyone. It had taken Brett Wallace only a decade to master the art of innocuousness. His own senseis—his teachers—would call it *mugei-mumei-jutsu,* the art of being anonymous. To them, and now to him, everything in life was an art. It was to be approached and treated as an art. In America Brett Wallace was the foremost artist, a *ninja* master.

But his standing as such had been seriously threatened by the rash act of one of his *chunin*—his lieutenants. There were three of them, all of whom he had trusted implicitly

61

until a few days ago. When Hama had disappeared along with his ceremonial sword, Wallace had turned all his sizeable investigative ability onto the mystery.

His state-of-the-art NEC computer illegally tapped into the city's lines. Every airline ticket sold was reported to Brett's monitor in the loft above The Rhea Dawn restaurant. He narrowed the field by turning Rhea's ample feminine charms on the taxi drivers in the area. Their memories were much sharper for a beautiful Japanese woman than they would be for a mediocre-looking man.

He had correctly assumed that Hama would be too anxious to take public transportation when a cab would be faster. Sure enough, one driver remembered dropping the squat bald Oriental off at the TWA terminal. Brett shifted through all the flights that were leaving at that time until he had a list of names Hama might be traveling under and a list of cities those names were destined for.

He set Jeff up in front of a companion console to check every news item in every listed city for any hint of Oriental overtones. Brett knew that a man reacted that way only in one instance—when a loved one was under threat. Jeff found the key splashed all over the front page of the *Daily News*. CHINATOWN FIRE CLAIMS TWENTY.

The names of the victims were withheld pending next-of-kin notification, but they lucked out when checking subsequent days' obituary listings. As soon as the name "Oshikata, Barbara" appeared, Brett booked a flight to New York City.

He continued researching on the plane. The police thought the club fire was gang related. A gang called the Killer B's had been emasculated several days later. Their main adversaries had been a Chinatown gang called the Tiger Claws. Their main hangout was the Sun Sung Cinema.

Brett rounded the corner of Bleeker Street to see his people at the corner cafe. They were sipping drinks under the modest marquee for the Bleeker Street Cinema. Brett smiled without much humor at the films showing today. Raizo Ichikawa as Kyoshiro Nemuri in the 1968 *Trail of Traps* and Shintaro Katsu as Zato Ichi in *The Blind Masseur's Cane Sword.*

Wallace walked right by his people and took a right. By the time he reached Houston Street, they were right behind him. Rhea walked in beauty, like the night. Even in the plain jeans and short-sleeved shirt, her Japanese grace and charm was unmistakable. Jeff made a good companion for her, looking as if he just got an athletic scholarship for some Ivy League college. He seemed younger than his twenty-seven years and had the tightly muscled body of a panther.

Anyone looking at the four would not have believed they were united in a partnership forged by tragedy and cemented by over five hundred years of military history. Schooled in the ancient arts of *ninjutsu,* Brett trained his *chunin* to fight alongside him, utilizing every skill in the human vocabulary. Rhea ran a Sausalito Japanese restaurant—The Rhea Dawn. Jeff taught at the Dawn Dojo martial arts school.

All that was nearly meaningless now in the face of Hama's loss. He had explained to the others how he had changed his name from Oshikata when he devoted his life to *ninjutsu.* He told them of his niece's brutal death and his irrational reaction to it. They all knew that the battle could be personal, but the fighting could never be. Not if you wanted to win.

To win necessitated a level of calm very few could achieve, a level of calm Brett had learned over ten years of training. But he could well understand Hama's pain. The road that led to his ninja mastery started with the dismemberment of his parents and the rape/murder of his pregnant wife. Brett could still feel their murderers' bodies being crushed beneath his onslaught.

But he did not want a scene of guilt and recrimination now. He knew Hama was aware of the situation. He had moved forward without thought or planning, risking exposure, which meant immediate death to a ninja. But their path had already been chosen by his enraged attacks. The only way out was by reaching the goal Hama had started toward.

"The girl Barbara Oshikata died in a Chinatown nightclub," Brett said, his lips hardly moving, his head still turned away from the others. "Chinatown is the territory of the Tiger Claws. The Tiger Claws' closest enemy were the Killer B's. They were the first to go. Why kill the Chinese?"

"I was convinced the American gang had not attacked the club," Hama replied simply, knowing that Brett would back him up. He was right. If the normally placid, affable man was certain the terrified Houston Street gang members were telling the truth, then it was believable.

"Why would the Chinese firebomb a club in their own territory?" he asked.

"There is a gang war of unprecedented scope going on," Hama answered. "The Tiger Claws could have wanted to frame the Killer B's so the other gangs would unite against them."

"Everyone is scrambling to come out on top," Jeff mused. "It's just possible the Chinese would be cunning and savage enough to do it."

"Could, would, possible, impossible," Rhea said with disgust. "No one has any facts, and the streets are getting bloodier."

"The city is better off without the gangs," Brett said evenly as the group turned the corner from Houston onto West Broadway. "But this kind of plotting seems beyond the abilities of the hoods." They walked in silence for two blocks before Brett slowed and nodded. "You were wise to come here," he told Hama as they reached the Oshikata co-op.

That's when the second floor exploded above them.

Chapter Seven

Glass and flame rained down on the sidewalk as Rhea and Hama fell into the street from the force of the concussion. Both Brett and Jeff hugged the wall as the worst of the detonation dissipated. Immediately Brett made a cup of his two hands, Jeff ran forward, and the ninja master vaulted his young *chunin* up to the shattered second-floor windows.

Archer leaped into the inferno as Brett wrenched open the front door. He jumped up the staircase three steps at a time toward the Oshikata apartment entrance. Jeff moved slowly forward through the remnants of the living room. All the cabinets were blown open and all the crockery smashed. The carpets were in flames and the furniture thrown over backward. Lying in front of the beaten counter was the smoldering body of Denise Oshikata.

Jeff checked her vital signs. Those that weren't blasted away were still. She had been killed instantly by the blast. He looked over to where the flames were most concentrated. Their entire component entertainment center had been destroyed, the plastic videotapes catching fire like grenades going off. Although all the separate pieces were broken, the only item completely obliterated was the videotape machine.

The flames licked up to the ceiling, effectively blocking Jeff's path to the other rooms. Such was not Brett's problem. He reached the second-floor landing and bound over the ball of flame that was eating up the entrance floor like a wave crawling up a beachhead. He landed in the bathroom doorway and pushed himself off toward the rear of the apartment.

He wasn't able to see because of the heat and smoke until he slammed against the closed study door. He could tell instinctively that it was locked. Without moving back Brett slammed both his palms against the obstruction. His concentrated strength ripped the bolt out of the wooden wall. The door slammed back, opening onto a scene from hades.

All the paraphernalia of Alex Oshikata's life was piled up around the rolltop desk against the left side wall. The papers, pictures, and memorabilia was stacked against and tacked to the wall—almost to the twelve-foot ceiling. Alex was standing away from his desk in the middle of the room.

He had been looking out the window on the far wall when Brett broke in. He whirled when the door slammed against the near wall. His mouth and eyes were open wide, making him look exactly like the dying Chinese boy who had taken his daughter out for that fateful date, up to and including the fact that both were on fire.

The entire room was engulfed in flames as if Brett had broken down the door of a furnace. The resulting blast hurled the ninja master backward, sending him right through the wall of fire that obstructed Jeff. He wrapped his arms around his head and slid across the floor on his back until he crashed into the collection of plants Denise had set near the windows.

He felt water splashing across his body and looked up to see Jeff spraying him with the sink hose from over the open-air kitchen counter. Brett ran back to the living room entrance, dove through the fire again, somersaulted

66

and tackled the immolated man. They both smashed through the den window and dropped the single story to the grassy ground.

Brett spun so that he was able to land rolling. He could do little to cushion Oshikata's fall, but he had to do what he could to save the man from the flames. They landed in a grass-covered oasis sandwiched between buildings. The various doors led out to the patio, and picnic furniture was strewn about the area.

Oshikata lay gasping on his back next to an umbrella table. Brett immediately went over and tried to reduce the pain with accupressure. The man seemed to breath easier, but when his smoking hands reached up for the sky his craterous eyes could not see.

"Hama," he gasped. "Hama . . . !"

Brett spoke to him soothingly in Japanese. "I am your brother's friend. He has avenged your daughter's death."

"No!" the man cried, his voice a tortured wheeze. "He has not. Not yet. You must promise . . . ! Swear. Swear you will punish our daughter's murderers!"

"I promise," Brett said immediately, with total conviction. "On my life and the lives of my ancestors."

Oshikata smiled, his broiled lips red and raw. "A woman," he choked. "A girl's voice on the phone . . ."

The dying man paused, his mouth working desperately, as if he couldn't get the words out or he couldn't make them understood.

"Yes," Brett urged. "Who was she? What did she say?"

Oshikata's last words were clear in the still night air. He lay smoldering on the cool grassy ground and recited the girl's message verbatim. Brett had never experienced a more macabre sensation as he listened.

"Rub a dub dub," Oshikata quoted. "Three men in a tub. And who do you think they be? A butcher, a baker, a candlestick maker . . . turn them out . . . knaves all three."

*   *   *

James Shin stood proudly admidst the skeleton of his new building. He stood on the center of three floors built over an underground parking garage and looked out over the East River from Sixty-Third Street. The early morning brought a certain peace to the city unlike no other time of day. Even the muggers were calling it a night when the blinding orange stabs of sunlight first appeared.

Shin looked away from the glistening river and back to the basic structure of his new dining establishment. Once this is ready, he thought, there'll be no more toiling in the business sweatshops of Chinatown. No more scrambling for customers, along with dozens of other restaurants all on the same street.

Now there'll finally be authentic Chinese dining on the Upper East Side, he reveled. With the incredible mass of young executives and their families living in the area, the Chinatown Club East was bound to be a success. And with the insurance money coming in, construction would move smoothly from here on in.

"Everything all right up there?" came the deep voice of his bodyguard.

"Fine, Mel," he called down without moving.

"Well . . ." the bodyguard almost groaned, "you going to be up there much longer?" Shin could practically see the man stretching with fatigue next to Shin's big black limousine, but he had to admire Mel's verbal style. The way he said it almost sounded as if Mel was more concerned about Shin's well-being than his own exhaustion.

"We'll see," Shin replied pointedly.

Mel grimaced and leaned up against the car fender. The window beside him opened with an electric hum. "How much longer?" said the tough-looking bruiser inside.

" 'We'll see,' he says," Mel said derisively, but quietly, while jerking his head toward the construction site.

"Great," the other guard sarcastically drawled.

"You better get out here," Mel suggested.

"What?" the man inside quietly exclaimed. "Are you

kidding? You can catch him if he falls. I'm staying right here." The man inside turned back to the issue of *Fortune* he was scanning.

Shin saw his own fortune spreading out before him. He had been nervous at first, but it looked like everything was going to work out after all. The Oriental businessman spread his arms wide, then clapped his palms together, rubbing them. "It can't miss," he said to himself with giddy pleasure. "It has to work."

"As long as the doors aren't locked," said a soft voice behind him.

Shin spun to stare directly into the rising sun's powerful first rays. He reared back, his arm coming up to shield his eyes.

"And as long as the water is working," the voice said.

Shin backed up in terror, his sun-stabbed vision frantically trying to locate the speaker. When he could see nothing but the thick wooden ceilings, wooden floors, and metal wall supports, he spun and ran for the makeshift stairway. Brett Wallace ran after him, stabbed the *kamayari* sickle-spear into the planks just behind Shin's foot and vaulted in front of the businessman.

A cloud seemed to pass before Shin's ears. He jumped back again, just barely making out a man-shaped figure in front of him draped in cloth the color of falling dust. In the dazzling new-day sun, it didn't look like a man at all, but a monster consisting of shifting sand.

Only, the weapon in his hand was real enough. It was a spear, a dull brown spear with two six-inch hooks tapering down toward the handle on either side of the arrow head. The hooks wouldn't dig in when the spear was used. They would serve as scythes when the spear was swung.

"Who are you?" Shin gasped. "What do you want?"

"A butcher, a baker, a candlestick maker," the shrouded figure before him said drily.

'What are you talking about?" Shin cried shrilly, his voice getting louder.

The spear spun in Brett's hand, the handle snaking behind Shin's ankle. With a tug he had knocked the businessman to the floor on his back. The fellow's perfectly tailored pinstripe suit got all dirty. As quickly as he had tripped him, Brett spun the *kamayari* back so the spear tip just touched the Oriental's many chins. He planted one foot on Shin's quivering chest.

"The emergency doors were padlocked shut," he said. "The emergency water supply had been turned off. You were home sick on the busiest night of the week. This fire wasn't a chance Tong attack."

"I don't know!" Shin babbled. "I swear! Oh, God, help! Help me someone!" The bodyguards didn't need any more coaxing. They scrambled into the construction site, pulling 9mm automatics from their shoulder holsters. One ran for the elevator while the other headed for the stairs.

Brett sliced a two-inch opening on Shin's jawline. The businessman gasped and clutched at the oozing blood. The ninja ran back to the open-air construction elevator shaft and leaped over its protective fencing. He dropped down to its roof just as it started to rise. He let the car feel his weight, jarring the bodyguard inside.

The gunman ran over to the opening to look up just as Brett swung the *kamayari* down between the bodyguard's jawline and neck. The sickle sunk deep and hooked into the man's jawbone. The pain was so great he couldn't scream or aim. Brett pulled him just off his feet so all he could do was wave his arms and legs as his face pumped blood down his suit.

The second bodyguard got up the stairs just as the elevator reached the second floor. He saw Brett on top, and there was nothing to keep him from shooting. His gun rose quickly, but not fast enough.

When the second man pulled the trigger, Brett had pulled the first guard up in front of himself as a shield. The 9mm hunk of lead plowed into the man's chest. He started in place like a shaken ragdoll, then collapsed as the elevator continued up to the fourth floor.

Mel stared in disbelief at his dead partner as the rising elevator carried him out of sight. His eyes were not on the crouching Brett Wallace, who appeared behind the elevator shaft as the car continued up. Before the elevator floor had even cleared his chin, he threw the *kamayari*.

It shot forward as if propelled by a crossbow. Almost as if the point were outfitted with a heat-seeking device, it plunged into the right side of Mel's chest—just missing his heart—and cracked through his spine, paralyzing him in place.

Brett casually walked forward with an easy gait. Shin gawked at him, then at Mel, who remained as motionless as a statue honoring ignominious death. Shin looked back at the slowly approaching Brett, then crawled frantically to the left.

Brett ignored him, choosing instead to stand before the already dead bodyguard. The ninja gripped his spear and pulled it out. Mel languidly drifted backward and fell down the stairs he initially had run up. Brett's eyes turned inexorably back toward Shin. The businessman was pulling himself up by the metal banister of the fire escape stairs, his own eyes staring wildly back.

The ninja came at him with a measured pace, the *kamayari* point low. It was a purposeful approach. Brett didn't like using the sickle-spear—it was too showy—but he knew the value of intimidation. He knew that Shin had struggled too long and too hard to give up his hopes for wealth and favor easily. It was quite possible the hysteric would let Brett kill him rather than admit any wrongdoing. For the Chinese the knowledge of infamy was one thing . . . the confession of guilt was entirely another.

So Brett had used the ancient ninja psychology of *kyosha-goyoku*—an exploitation of the basic human desire for self-preservation. The Japanese, sometimes to

71

their shame, were masters of this. Attacking Oriental hordes would warn an enemy only once, then slaughter everything in their path, leaving huge mounds of decapitated heads in their wake. Tales of this savagery would preceed them so that the initial threat was enough to secure surrender.

Brett needed to show Shin what he could do and what could easily happen to him before the man would loosen up. The restaurateur looked ready to say absolutely anything as Brett neared the fenced-in fire escape. A dark chain-link network covered the whole metal stairway like a wall, preventing Shin from escaping until he reached the first unfinished floor.

The terrified man rocked from side to side as he stumbled down the steps, his hands blindly reaching for an escape that wasn't there. Brett came after him a spear length behind. Finally Shin had reached the last step. He triumphantly leaped forward to push open the emergency exit and escape into the morning light.

The door held fast. It had been locked from the outside.

Shin spun in numb horror. He stared into the face of an avenging demon, a face that had no features, his hellish trident held before him.

"A girl called me," he blurted. "A girl said I could make a lot of money if I just did what I was told."

"Who was the girl?"

"I don't know!" Shin maintained. "I swear! She just told me what to do over the phone."

"The money," Brett urged him on.

"It was in a cabbage crate with the next morning's delivery! Five thousand dollars! That's all I know, I promise! I swear on the life of my ancestors . . ."

Brett pushed the spear blade into the man's heart with a quick thrust. He didn't want his vow to Oshikata cheapened by showing any mercy to a man who let twenty innocent people die horribly in order to advance himself. He pulled the *kamayari* loose, wiped the blood on Shin's white shirt, then kicked the locked door open.

His pent-up frustration was more than enough to break the simple combination lock. The metal door swung loose, and Brett moved quickly to the rented car waiting for him. Jeff drove down the empty street to East End Avenue. Hama turned in the passenger seat to look at Brett as he pulled the ninja hood off.

"Anything?"

"No accidents," Brett reported. "They were no accidents. None of them. The firebombing at the Chinatown club was planned well in advance."

"Even street gangs plan," Jeff worried. "They don't do everything on sudden impulse."

"They don't do *anything* with five-thousand-dollar bribes, either," Brett countered, pulling off his leggings to reveal well-worn jeans beneath. "Someone's paying for a lot of death."

"That doesn't mean the Oshikata killings were connected," Rhea mused.

"All connected," Brett said with assurance. "The restaurant attack was professional. The Oshikata attack was professional."

Brett remembered the burning study. Any thought of accident was dispelled by that sight. The fire had flared up in two places: the living room and den. That meant only one thing—flamboyant arson. Arson perpetrated by a firebug with imagination and amorality. The Baker.

"But why?" Hama said with pain coloring his voice. "It still doesn't explain why!"

"One line," Brett said brutally, looking directly into Hama's tortured eyes. "There is one line connecting the Chinatown club and the Oshikata co-op. One girl called Shin with the bribe. One girl called Alex Oshikata with a perverted warning." The ninja master leaned forward.

73

"There was only one girl you left alive at Jonathan Dunne's apartment."

The silence inside the car was deafening and bottomless. The things that kept Hama from losing his grip were his ninja training and the fact that the Oshikatas' lives were already shattered by their daughter's death. Their own deaths came as a release from a pain almost as great as their daughter Barbara's.

'But," Hama finally choked out, "how could they have traced me?"

"They didn't need to," Brett continued, not trying to be cruel. "All they had to know was the attacker was an Oriental with a grudge against both Occidentals and Chinese. Once the list of the dead was released, they played it safe by going back and getting the Japanese."

"Incredible," Jeff breathed.

"Just one more story in the Naked City," Rhea said sadly. She had spent too much time indexing unbelievably ugly crimes out of Brett's computerized information system to be surprised by anything.

"Who are they?" Hama asked quietly, his head turned away.

"That is what we're going to find out," Brett said with certainty. "Whoever it is will know that an Oriental avenger is on the loose and working his way up the list of suspects. They'll know because a girl named Connie C. told them. They'll know because the innocent bystanders at the Sun Sung Cinema will tell them. They'll know because the *kamayari* marks in Shin and his bodyguards will tell them.

"All we have to do is keep moving until they come for us."

"And when they do . . ." Hama intoned, his teeth grinding against each other.

"And when they do, Hama . . ." Brett echoed, waiting until the man turned back and their eyes locked. The or-

74

iental's features were intense. His master's face was expressionless.

"And when they do," the ninja master instructed plainly, "no pity."

Chapter Eight

The intersection of Broadway and Bleeker was extraordinarily common. Common because there were many intersections like it in New York. Extraordinary because the roads in four directions led to completely different immediate environments. Go south and Broadway would lead to Chinatown. Go east and Bleeker went right into the heart of Greenwich Village. Go north to find the heart of midtown Manhattan.

But go west young man, and the road would lead to a section of slum at the corner of Crosby Street. Crosby Street hardly befitted Bing's namesake, given that it was a stretch of cobblestone road hardly longer than a football field fenced in on either side by rundown warehouses.

It emptied from Bleeker onto Houston, and the wide asphalt and concrete expanse was littered with garbage of all sorts. There were cans, drums, and dumpsters of garbage that seemed to be refuse-spewing machines rather than receptacles. They were always full, and remnants were always blowing or rolling in the wind that surged through the manmade canyon like an invisible sea.

Connie Chesinski stumbled among the papers and cans in front of an upraised loading door. She looked good from a distance. At a distance all one might see is a slim girl with short, boyishly cut blond hair, wearing tight designer jeans and a horizontally striped long-sleeved V-neck pullover.

It was only close up that one might notice her pale complexion under the hastily put-on makeup, the slight vibration of her neck and folded arms, and the hesitation in her walk that wasn't entirely due to the awkwardness of her high-heeled sandals. She hugged herself as if cold in the hot, humid night, teetering on the edge of a pool of light made by one of the four lampposts positioned along the abortive street.

From a distance one could see her mouth working. Up close one could hear clear words. "Sing a song of six packs, a bottle full of rye," she sang under her breath. "Four and twenty blackbirds baked in a sty. When the sty was opened, the birds began to sing. Wasn't that a dandy dish to set before the queen . . . ?"

"Hey mama, what you singing there?"

Chesinski's head snapped up, swinging to the right to peer into the darkness next to a dumpster. Out of the gloom walked a slight black man wearing a Con-Funk-Tion tour jacket with no shirt underneath.

"C.W.," she sighed. "It's you."

"Who were you expecting, baby?" he asked. "Bill Cosby with a pudding pop? What you singing there?"

"Nothing, C.W., nothing," she said, moving over to him. She walked like an old woman with an advanced case of arthritis. Her back was bent, and her torso twisted to the side. At this range fat beads of sweat covering her brow could be discerned. "I've got to talk to you."

Clyde Winslow Nelson gave a low whistle at his first clear sight of her. "You sure do, honey," he said. "You surely do." If there was anything he disliked more than addicts with the shakes, it was his own name. Trust his wimp parents to give him a jive name like Clyde Winslow. So everybody either called him "C.W." or they became

78

the proud new owners of a six-inch switchblade gash across their faces.

"I need some bad," Connie said unnecessarily.

"So you said on the phone," Nelson reminded her. "What's the matter darling? Johnny Stick no longer putting out for you? Or was it the other way around?"

The mention of her late boyfriend was enough to straighten Connie's spine—a move she came to regret in the next second. "God damn it, C.W.," she groaned, her back bending again. "You know what happened. I haven't been able to score anything since then."

"I sure hope you been able to score some other kind of Johns," the pusher said. "Or else you ain't gonna be able to afford anything I got."

Connie saw in his face that it wasn't going to be a handout for old time's sake. "Hell, you know I've been hiding out," she said in the most reasonable voice she could muster. She tried to straighten again in a pathetic attempt to look sensual. "But maybe you and I could make up for lost time." She reached up to caress his cheek.

He slapped her hand away. "You know I don't do it with junkies."

The vamping veneer was stripped away by her sudden rage and desperate need. "Damn you!" she screamed, coming at him with both hands up, fingernails out like claws. "Damn you to hell!"

Two big black hands shot forward out of the darkness behind Nelson and grabbed Connie's wrists in midmotion. A huge bald muscle man in jeans and a fish-net shirt was on the other end of these muscular arms. His face was a placid mask of dark-skinned bumps, and his deep-set eyes carried enough threatening warning to melt the wicked witch of the West on the spot.

C.W. laughed. "Hell, bitch, you know I never go nowhere's without Ritchie." The pusher clucked in mock sympathy. "You know better than that." The hulking

79

guard let go of Chesinski's hands while pushing her back. The girl staggered on the heels and rubbed her wrists. She frowned, unable to think of anything to do or say.

C.W. solved the conversation problem. He smiled and snapped his fingers. Out of the shadows came three other black bruisers, each looking as strong and dangerous as Ritchie.

"Hey," Connie said with a nervous laugh. "What's the army for C.W.? I didn't bring anybody along."

"No," C.W. said musically, moving forward. "Of course not, baby. But I just wanted to make sure you didn't give me no trouble, you know?"

Connie started backing up, her cold-turkey shakes suddenly forgotten. "Trouble?" she echoed. "What kind of trouble could I give you, C.W.?"

"You been telling tales out of school, honey-chile," he smiled, getting closer. "There's some folks that don't much like that."

"What you talkin' 'bout?" Chesinski asked uncertainly, knowing exactly what he was talking about but not how he knew. "I didn't do nothin'!"

"No, no, baby," C.W. said, getting within arm's length. "You got that wrong. It's 'I won't do nothin'.'"

Chesinski bleated when C.W. Nelson grabbed her arm. With a hand tug he threw the weakened girl to the arms of the men behind him. She fell among the four brawny blacks with a feeble struggle. The only thing that was strong was her voice, which she used as best she could while trying to climb out of the dark tree of muscular limbs.

"What do you know?" she half pleaded, half accused. "You don't know nothing! You're just a lousy pusher!"

The four blacks securely held her writhing body and started carrying her toward the warehouse. C.W. walked alongside, conversing affably with the girl as if she were on a train leaving the station and he was keeping pace along side. "I'm known in this town, sugar," he said. "Whenever

80

anybody wants anything, they come to me, dig? You came, right?"

"It's a lie, C.W.!" she countered. "I didn't do anything! They can't prove anything!"

"They don't have to prove anything to me, sweets," C.W. said before Ritchie kicked open the door of the warehouse and carried her inside. "Their money did all the talking for them." He closed the door behind him; then the quartet of blacks plus one moved into total darkness.

Connie Chesinski drifted on that cloud of darkness both in mind and body. For the last twelve hours the demons in her mind had been content to just scream at her for more dope. Only now they were starting to spray-paint the walls. In the blackness she could only hope that all her troubles would disappear.

The hanging overhead lamp brought her back to reality. It clicked on, emitting a pool of pale yellow light that spotlighted a plain metal chair on the floor of a simple office cubicle. The chair was positioned before a worn metal desk. Behind that was a blackboard and a pointer. Next to that was a wooden pole that was used to open the warehouse's large bulletproof windows—the kind that swung down, not opened up or out.

Ritchie slammed the girl onto the seat. One man took one of the girl's arms each and held them securely to the arms of the chair. The third man stood behind her, his hands clamping down on her shoulders. C.W. picked up the blackboard pointer while Ritchie leaned his haunches against the desk edge and folded his arms.

Connie's eyes moved about wildly, the sweat now pouring out of her entire body. It made her skin slippery, but the blacks still held her nice and tight. C.W. walked toward her, lightly tapping the pointer's rubber tip in his palm.

"C.W., I swear," she said, "I didn't do anything wrong. I made a phone call, sure. But I didn't give anything away. It was a joke, that's all. One lousy call, and I was

81

just jiving him, you know? Just making it worse for him, you know?"

Nelson stopped in front of her, his face twisted in thought. "What you talking about, woman?" he said irritably. "I don't know nothing about no fucking phone call."

The girl thought he was only trying to make it worse for her. "Please, C.W., please, don't do this to me. You've got it all wrong!"

The pusher's expression went from sadistic anticipation to cunning delight. "What I got all wrong, darling? You tell me about it."

Chesinski sucked her breath in. She finally realized that Nelson didn't know anything about the taunting phone call to Oshikata. Suddenly she realized that he wasn't here to kill her for that; he was here to kill her on general principles. She was a loose end, a weak link. The Butcher wanted her dead——just in case, and he had gone to the one person he knew Connie would have to contact sooner or later.

Only now that contact saw a way of getting more cash out. If he knew what Connie didn't want the Butcher to know, he could get a long-term ticket on the blackmail train. Torturing her would be twice as much fun now. "Come on, baby," he said, raising the thin wooden pointer like a whip. "Tell Uncle C all about it."

The man behind her gripped the sides of her shirt's V-neck and neatly tore the cloth down the middle. Connie groaned and twisted under the others' hands. The man behind her then reached across and tore the shirt completely off her torso from the bottom up.

Her pale, shining flesh gleamed in the light, the sweat giving it radiance. Her breasts were somewhat small, but well-rounded and strong as her chest heaved. Her rib cage appeared and disappeared over her tight stomach muscles as she gulped air.

C.W.'s eyes left her face, and all thought of extra money left his brain for the moment. He almost bit his lip, then brutally swung the pointer. The wood shaft sung in the air of the huge warehouse before it slammed against her breasts with a loud cracking noise.

Connie gasped, surprised that a stinging pain could be layered on top of the excruciating cold-turkey ache. She never knew how much she could be hurt before. Nelson didn't give her time to recover. The pointer flew in again and again, leaving red welt-encrusted marks to show where it had hit.

The singing wood became a dull hum punctuated by sizzling crackles, then high-pitched grunts and gasps. "Come on baby, light my fire," C.W. said in rhythm with his strokes. "You let me know when you're ready to talk."

Chesinski tried desperately not to speak. She figured she was in bad enough trouble already. In her addled mind, telling C.W. about the call would only make things worse. So she groaned between clenched teeth as Nelson made her chest look like a meatball pizza.

Finally she could stand it no longer. It seemed as if he had been beating her for at least ten minutes although the pointer had only been raking her flesh for three. Her chest felt as if all the skin had been peeled off and he was meeting the raw meat beneath. The pain licked up her middle like fire, slicing into her brain through her neck.

Still, she refused to let him break her. She would give him no satisfaction. Her lips parted, her teeth unclenched, but no screams emerged. No confession poured out. Instead she began babbling quietly, as if chanting a mantra or mumbling a prayer. As the sound of the wooden reed whipping her served as counterpoint, she recited her warped nursery rhymes.

"Mary, Mary, quite contrary, how does your garden grow . . . with cockle shells and baby bells and three lips all in a row. . . . High diddle diddle, the cat and the fiddle,

83

the dog jumped over the moon . . . the women all laughed to see such sport and the babe ran away with the goon. . . ."

The quiet chanting finally threw off C.W.'s concentration. He pulled the pointer back and leaned in. "What you saying, baby?"

"This little biggy went to Martha. . . ."

"I can't hear you, honey-chile."

"This little biggy played with his bone. . . ."

"Say what?"

"This little biggy had roast feet. . . ."

C.W. straightened and signaled Ritchie to come over.

"This little biggy had fun. . . ."

Ritchie handed him the cardboard container that had the words "When It Rains, It Pours" inscribed on it. C.W. poured some of the white powder into his cupped hand.

"And this little biggy went wee-wee all over his . . ."

The pusher slapped the salt onto Connie's bleeding chest.

The girl screamed with chilling sound and echoing volume. She bucked against the six huge hands that held her with strength she never thought she possessed. She squirmed and squealed as the salt ate into her wounds. C.W. needed to help hold her down. Her mouth was level with his head so he got the worst of her shrieking right in his ear.

"Keep her quiet, will ya?" he seethed at Ritchie, who hovered just behind her. "Shut her up."

Ritchie seemed to have boy scout blood in him, because out of his jacket came a dark blue rubber ball and a roll of packing tape. With one hand he grabbed Connie's jaw. He squeezed it so that his fingers dug under her jaw bone. With the other he stuffed the ball in her mouth, prying it wide.

The screams diminished to explosive grunts as Chesinski strove to keep sane. Once the initial shock ended, a buzz-saw sensation overwhelmed her, as if African ants

84

were making a smorgasbord of her torso. As she suffered, Ritchie plastered two large hunks of tape over her lips to keep the ball inside.

C.W. Nelson smiled at his guard's handiwork. Just then Connie's leg jerked up, as if her tormenter had been testing her reflexes. Her knee sunk into C.W.'s testicles.

Nelson doubled over and stumbled back, both hands cupped over the enflamed area. His dark face grew a shade of purple, and his mouth puckered to the size of a grape pit.

Chesinski, in the meantime, was oblivious to what she had done. She continued to writhe in the chair, her eyes tightly closed. The horrors inside her head were bad enough; she wouldn't have been able to take the persistence of this vision.

The pusher gasped, choked, and caught his breath. He straightened up slowly, blinking his eyes against the tears that streamed out. He looked at the quaking girl, red veins slowly appearing outside his pupils. If looks could kill, Chesinski would have learned the harp by now.

C.W. reached into his coat pocket and began putting on his skintight, butter-soft leather gloves. Ritchie knew what that meant. Nelson was about to move in for the kill. He was going to methodically batter this white junkie, reveling in every bruise, until he had turned her head into Grey Poupon. The number one bodyguard moved back, allowing his boss a clear shot to the squirming, sniveling girl.

C.W. moved forward until he was right in front of Chesinski. Let her kick now. He'd break her legs for her. He took one last look at the once pretty girl. Her nose was running. The bags under her eyes were taking on the colors of the American Flag. The once clear skin was blemished with black heads and blotched with discoloration.

He wanted to remember her as she was right now. For in a few minutes she'd never look that way again C.W.

85

Nelson's muscles tensed. His fingers slowly curled into tight fists. His arm drew back.

Brett Wallace slipped down from his position atop the cubicle's low wall and landed soundlessly nine feet behind the pusher. He somersaulted and came up quickly. His right leg swung up with the speed and power of a professional place kicker, slamming his granite-like foot right between Nelson's legs.

The pusher lifted off the floor like a Space Shuttle shot. He flew forward like a human cannonball—completely over the heads of his bodyguards, drifted lazily over the back of Chesinski's torture chair and smashed through the glass of the office door upside down. He crashed to the floor outside, pushing glass shards deep inside his torso.

Doctors later would be unable to tell what killed him first: the glass blades or the fact that his private parts looked like three-alarm chili.

Wallace was sorry they had gagged her. It was quite possible that in her present delirious state she might have said something he wanted to know. That was why he had waited this long to move in. He didn't enjoy watching her being tortured, but it was necessary. He learned to do whatever was necessary over his many years of hardship.

Many heroes would have rushed in to save the damsel in distress as soon as any hint of danger cropped up. That was why there were so many dead heroes. Instead Brett had watched, waited, and listened. She had done too much evil and he had spent too much time tracking her down to let her get off easy.

In the leased Bethune apartment Rhea had arranged through the Dawn Corporation, before they left, Brett had unpacked the Nippon Electric portable computer with modem. He lifted the Touch-Tone phone receiver, pushed the talking and listening end into the rubber holders, and stabbed the phone buttons in a rhythmic, unusual pattern.

It had taken him two years, but now Brett had the

"number" of almost every major police computer in the country. With the modem unit, he could have his Sausalito computer talk to the NYPD computer, then transmit the information back to Bethune Street. The words came out as little dots—matrix letters—on a roll of paper.

The police machine reported that Connie Chesinski had been arrested several times on drug and prostitution charges. Her basic connection to both was Clyde Winslow Nelson. His hangouts were centered around the A Street area. With Rhea, Jeff, Hama, and Brett on the street, it was only a matter of time before they spotted him.

In fact it took three hours and forty-five minutes. Archer reported in, directed Brett to the Lodestone Bar on Lafayette Street, and Wallace took it from there. Jeff went back to the apartment to continue Hama's crash course in the more extreme arts of *ninjutsu*.

Brett shadowed Nelson for the rest of the day. As night came on he took a moment to pull off his street clothes, throw them away, and slip up his hood, which looked like a kerchief under his now discarded shirt. The pusher made his way to Crosby, where the others met him. Connie wasn't far behind.

Ritchie and Nelson's other men stared at their dying boss and then back at the spot the attack came from. They could see absolutely nothing outside the dim yellow border of the hanging lamp. Ritchie quickly reached inside his jacket and pulled out a Smith and Wesson 9mm automatic, model 439. He pointed the four-inch barrel at the seemingly empty space and pulled the trigger three times.

The powerful gun boomed in the open space, the bullets smashing into the wood wall beyond. The echo bounced off the cavernous walls of the building for a few seconds as the three men holding Chesinski down blinked and Ritchie peered carefully into the gloom.

The gun's flashing reports had lit the space momentarily. He had watched carefully and seen nothing. All his senses told him that Nelson had propelled himself through the door behind them, but no one could jump that far from a standing position even if they wanted to.

Ritchie suddenly looked at the still wriggling, still moaning Connie in something close to fear. He had seen the movie *Carrie*. Was it possible . . . ?

Wallace decided to come down from atop the hanging lamp at that point. The black thugs hadn't seen him jump up there, and they didn't see him come down either. The ink-black ninja uniform that exposed only his eyes took care of most of the subterfuge. Brett's painting of the skin around his eyes black and his *ninjutsu* took care of the rest.

Ritchie walked into the darkness totally confused. His fellows watched in equal confusion. Suddenly their vision was marred by what looked like three flashes—as if someone had just taken their picture thrice. They felt a sudden strange flush in rapid succession. Ritchie turned around to look at them.

He was just in time to see their hands separate from their arms.

Brett moved back, his sword held down, to keep away from the six fountains of crimson liquid that burst free of the guards' limbs. He had quickly and neatly guillotined the trio's wrists with three quick chops of the samurai blade.

He had let the speed and power of the initial attack on the left man spin the sword around, pivoting his body so the sword started its second circle over the right man's wrist. The third turn was redirected so that Brett rolled through the air with the sword and landed between the right man and the one behind. Then he just brought the blade down from the *dai-jodan* position—directly over his head—cutting the third man's wrists.

He stood placidly, the sword in the *gedan* position—point lowered—as the trio of torturers wandered frenetically around. Ritchie ran forward, his mouth agape, helpless as they were to do anything. His men were screaming in pain and fear, their arms blood hoses that sprayed the room with the grafitti of death.

Ritchie found himself turning his head slowly toward Chesinski again. She seemed unaware of her release. Her arms were spasmodically covering her rent chest. She was jerking in the chair as if electrified.

Ritchie's imagination totally got the better of him. He thought that her spasms were being brought on by her own psychic strength. He thought she had *made* his head look at her. He thought she was tearing everyone apart with her mind.

He raised the 9mm automatic quickly, hoping to blow her head off before she could do the same to him.

Ritchie was fast, but he wasn't fast enough. Brett performed *iai*—the sword quick-draw. His sword rose faster than Ritchie's gun arm. It was coming down just before the black man's finger tightened. Brett stepped forward, and the *katana* blade sunk through the thickest part of Ritchie's upper arm.

The black man's muscle mound was cut in half. Three-quarters of the arm fell to the floor, it's fingers still twitching. Ritchie watched as his mind's order was completed a split second too late. The gun fired, its bullet making a mouse hole in the opposite wall.

The other men had already fallen. Ritchie stared in wonder at his missing arm and diffidently tried to stem the blood flow with his good hand. Brett bent down and picked up the salt container Nelson had dropped. He walked toward Connie with it. Just before he sidled past the guard, he jerked his wrist, sending a hunk of potassium chloride into Ritchie's open wound.

It was like dumping a match into a gas tank. Ritchie exploded off the ground, slammed back first onto the office desk, somersaulted backward, and crashed into the wall.

Brett used acupressure on the suffering girl. It worked

89

as an anesthetic, so she felt nothing when he pulled the tape from her mouth even though it ripped skin off her parched lips. He could dam up the ache, but he could not temper her nervous system entirely. She was feeling no pain, but she was still flying high. Her pupils were the size of microdots.

"Talk to me," he said.

Connie just laughed, adrift inside her head.

"How did you know the Oshikatas would be killed?" he pressed. "What's your connection to all the killings?"

Connie sighed and started to coo.

Brett knew she would not respond to anything coherent. To get through, he'd have to go down to her level. "Rub a dub dub . . . ," he prompted.

That got a rise out of her. Chesinski's eyes opened, and her lips widened in a smile. She shook her finger at the black-garbed man with a knowing grin.

"Paddy cake. Paddy cake," she said. "Baker's man. Bake me a cake as fast as you can."

All the lights in the warehouse came on.

Chapter Nine

Damn New York anyway. With all the street noises, Brett's usually sharp sixth senses were dulled. He cursed himself for not being aware of whatever else was inside the warehouse with them.

Even as he was doing that, he was rectifying matters. His eye muscles tightened, keeping the surroundings in clear focus with just a blink. Whoever decided to let there be light would need at least a few seconds to become accustomed to the sudden change in illumination.

In those few seconds Brett saw all he needed to. The warehouse was a box interrupted by roofless cubicles and framed by a balcony that ran the length and width of the outermost walls. Standing on that balcony were a gang of street toughs.

It looked like the forces had been mobilized. The Butcher had used Chesinski as bait for the oriental avenger, and he was making sure the somewhat undependable pimp/pusher Nelson was taken care of after getting the addicted girl out of hiding.

The hoods started pouring down the stairs and lowering themselves down from the overhang when Brett dove to the side, barreled over the desk in a *soku ho kaiten* shoulder roll, and sprung off the desk edge so that he landed solidly on his feet without stepping on Ritchie's corpse.

At the exact moment his soles touched the floor, Brett's left hand snaked out to grasp the window pole. Then his knees straightened and he threw himself over the desk backward, twisting in midair so that he landed where he had originally started, facing Connie with the pole in his hand.

The window opening stick was just a makeshift replacement for a *bisen-to*—a staff ending in a blade. It felt completely natural in Brett's hands, like extensions of his arms. He twisted it beneath the hanging light brim and shattered the bulb with its tip. Chesinski didn't seem to notice that glass shards were raining down on her. She wasn't noticing anything.

Using the hook that grappled the window rings like a can opener, he twisted it between the bulb's metal screw and the lamp's receptor. He popped the broken bulb out like a cork from a wine bottle. Brett ignored the oncoming street gang, but he was perfectly aware of them. He knew how close they were by vibrations of their foot falls coming through the wooden floor.

Brett jammed the window stick's metal tip into the naked socket. The lights flickered from the surge of power, then died. The warehouse was plunged into darkness once more. Brett heard the yells of anger the hoods made, allowing him to place them in the gloom.

As he pivoted toward the broken door, he reached into a well-padded pouch on his hip. He pulled out some *tetsu-bishi* and threw them through the broken window of the door. The hoods in the lead ran right into them. Tiny pyramids bathed in poison, four-pointed caltrops sank through the creeps' shoes and into the flesh of their feet.

Brett heard their shouts of surprise and their bodies falling as he gripped the girl's arms. With a quick tug Connie Chesinski was folded over his shoulder. Her mind held important facts, but he needed her alive in order to discover them. And considering the way Nelson and company had acted, she was a lot safer with him than left there.

Brett bounded across the room in three steps and made an incredible leap to the top of the standing cubicle wall. Although it had no ceiling to get in his way, Brett had to use all his legs and arm muscles to get over. All his knowledge of *karumijutsu* was required to lighten himself so he could get the girl to the top of the eight-foot wall.

His legs stretched, then pulled in as he soared up, his toes gripped the air like fingers. The hand that wasn't holding the girl to his back grabbed the wall top and pulled his body up higher. Brett's soles just touched the wall's apex, and then he dropped noiselessly to the floor beyond—the cubicle between him and the surviving gang members.

They trampled over the bodies of their fellow gang members to get into the room, only to find it empty after frenzied searching. In the meantime Brett ran to the warehouse's front wall, looking for the best exit.

There was a growing roar outside, as if a huge tractor-trailer truck was rumbling ever closer. Without much consideration Brett pulled open the door Nelson had entered and leaped out onto Crosby Street.

There was a four-story building directly across the way. From the size of its shuttered grated windows, it could have been a very strict school or a very lax correctional facility. Out of its large double-front doors and down its chipped-stone steps were pouring a platoon of street fighters, all armed with the stuff that rumbles are made of.

Brett could not be sure they didn't see him as he moved behind the dumpster just outside the warehouse. The four lampposts shed enough light to make the black ninja uniform discernible. He tossed Chesinski inside the dumpster so they could not see her nestled among the trash, then moved quickly to the left side to confront the two

93

early birds. They had charged out of the opposite building, seemingly anxious to lead the way.

Years of street living had taken their toll. Both boys were thin, the first one was blond. Using a blindingly fast *iai* out of the scabbard on his back, Brett smashed the butt of his sword handle onto the blond's head. The ninja ducked as the kid fell forward. At the same time, Brett took the blade in his left hand and slashed it across the other guy's midsection.

As he straightened with the blond draped across his back, the other boy fell writhing to the gutter, his stomach sliced open. His screams brought the others running in that direction. Brett moved back to his right behind the dumpster. Twisting one arm behind his back, he grabbed the unconscious boy's vest and pulled it off the blond's otherwise naked torso. With the other arm he pulled off the kid's sneakers.

Brett came around the left side of the dumpster, seeing a path to the building the mob had come out of. Without hesitating he ran toward its entrance. He might have made it without obstruction if the gang members inside the warehouse hadn't finally made their way to the door.

The throng that had charged across the street was staring in confusion at their charge leader, who bucked in the gutter, his hands unable to sew his sliced stomach back together again. His screeching was enough to drown out Brett's progress at first.

But the others kicked open the warehouse door and saw Brett's back immediately. To their eyes the short-haired, shirtless blond upon it was still Chesinski. Their shouts and pointing finally caught the others' eyes and ears.

The blond was lying across his sword, and Brett needed a longer range than its blade anyway. He reached inside his shirt and pulled out the *manriki-gusari,* an eight-foot chain with sharpened, poisoned heavy spikes at both ends.

As soon as it reached his fingers, his hand started it spinning almost automatically. His feet slapped onto the stone steps, and his body rose toward the opening in the squat four-story building. Once inside, he might be able to lose himself in the labyrinth of rooms, escape out a back window, and return later for Chesinski.

His luck ran out on the fourth step. The growling roar of the gang behind him drowned out the sound of more thugs just inside the building's entrance. The stone beneath his feet swallowed up the vibrations of their movements. If he hadn't been the ninja master, he would have run directly into their arms.

Instead the *manriki-gusari* flashed up, one end wrapping around a broken flagpole that jutted out from the second-story ledge. The end of the chain link encircled the jagged shaft just long enough to support his weight as his feet left the front-door landing and he swung through the air.

It wasn't with the greatest of ease, but it would do until a trapeze came along. Brett's legs lashed out, pushing the compact group of attackers back inside the building. The force of the kicks stopped him dead in the air. He landed back on the porch-like landing, his profile to both the door and the street.

As the others fell, the first of the opposite street fighters came up the steps after him. He pulled down the flagpole tip of the weighted chain in a swinging arc. Like a fist on a long thin arm, the *manriki-gusari* blade swung across the faces of the second wave of attackers, splitting them open like a chain-saw Frisbee.

They fell back into the men just behind them, making the third wave crawl over their writhing bodies to reach the stairs. Brett wasn't waiting for them. With the savagery and resources of youth, the thugs inside the building bounced back from Brett's initial kicks quickly. In their haste to get at him, the first three men wedged themselves into the door frame.

In just a moment more they would have burst out, but Brett didn't let the time go. The *manriki* came around to wrap the ninja's outstretched arm, his hand still holding the other end. His fingers curled around the weighted spike as the other settled on his upper arm. Using the heavy blade like a combination baseball and spear, Brett threw the unwrapped end with all his might at the doorway.

His arm straightened, and the chain unraveled like kite thread off a spool. The spike tip all but exploded through the first thug's thin body and continued through another's. The point-blank momentum was enough to burst through the next one's back and bury itself in the stomach of a third.

A fourth danced back as his companions howled in pained surprise. The *manriki* had hardly stopped when Brett grabbed the other end before it left his arm and yanked back. The spike ripped out the way it had come, hurling the thugs forward. Brett swung the chain in a hard arc to the right, cutting down some more street people as the dying ones who had been inside fell down the steps, further blocking the way.

Brett let the chain go as it completed its second sweep. It slammed against the front-window grate and wrapped around the wire mesh there. He had all but forgotten it as he leaped through the front door. The man who avoided the spike came at him with a hunting knife. Brett lowered his shoulder so the blond took the blow.

The knife sunk into the kid's back between his shoulder blades. With just a roll of his own shoulder muscles, Brett catapulted the now dead boy atop his killer. Both fell to the ground. As the two fell Brett emptied the remainder of his *tetsu-bishi* across the inside of the doors.

Brett moved deeper into the building, assimilating its interior as he went. There was a room to his immediate left and right. They were empty of furnishings except for

96

debris. Their ceilings were high and their floors uneven.

There was a wooden staircase in front of him, taking up the right-hand side of the wide entry hall. There was a small pantry entrance on the left side of the hall and a narrow passage going to the east and west under the stairs. Brett wanted to eliminate as many of the attackers as possible before hazarding the floors above.

He moved into the room to his left quickly as the street mob fell over each other to get inside. The first few sank right onto the moat of caltrops before the others got wise. They started leaping across the patch of poisoned pyramids like seasoned paratroopers.

Brett slid his feet along the floor as if he were ice-skating. He maintained a respectable speed, but it was a good way to avoid any booby traps the thugs might have left. As he went, waiting for the new first wave to catch up, one part of his mind considered the predicament.

Connie C. got in touch with Nelson. Nelson had been contacted by the Butcher. Nelson arranges to kill Chesinski. Butcher arranges to back up the pusher. It now didn't seem likely that the hoods were there to kill C.W. The Butcher didn't need a school building full of thugs to do that.

No wonder Nelson took his time torturing the girl. She was just bait for the Oriental avenger that Hama, Connie, and Brett had—knowingly or unknowingly—transpired to create. The street mob was positioned to make sure the avenger didn't survive his rescue mission. It's just that they weren't counting on a modern-day ninja.

Brett felt a half-dozen more hoods nearing him. To them he was just a black shape vaguely outlined by the whitewashed walls. They ignored the fact that his shape seemed to shift everytime he moved. They went after him like they went after everything in their lives—with unreasoning hatred.

Brett counted on their stupid anger, but did not underestimate their cunning, speed, or intent. Like insane animals, they were not perfectly predictable. He'd have to work fast and at a fever pitch. Each of his attacks would have to be all out. There would be no giving quarter if he wanted to emerge unscathed, not to mention alive.

Brett's running feet stopped dead just before he reached the door to the narrow hallway. As he stopped, the blade streaked out of his back scabbard. To those coming quickly up behind, the blade did not stop moving or change direction. Shining in the moonlight, the sword swung around in one powerful movement.

The thug directly behind Brett tried to stop. He was unable to prevent his feet sliding right into the blade's path. His right arm went up to block the blow. The sword went right through that arm, through his neck, and lopped off three fingers from his other hand.

Brett struck without a sound. While others would be screaming martial arts yells, Wallace had developed his *ki*—his internal power—to such a level that his energy-building shout, his *kiai,* was intrinsic. The only sound the ninja made was the sound of his samurai sword whistling through the air.

The sound of the hood's arm and head being sliced off was a splashing thunk. Both parts spun in the air and bounced across the floor. The fingers skittered across the room, resounding like bouncing Tootsie Rolls. The body stood in place for an awkward second, then was rooted to the spot by twin spurts of blood coming out of the rended elbow and neck.

Only then did the body fall back. And only after it had hit the floor did the others realize that the ninja had disappeared from behind it.

That slowed the savages somewhat. But as soon as they rounded the widening pool of blood, their momentum picked up again. It was as if they had forgotten about the man's incredible death as soon as they passed him.

Their comrades had died before. They were all biodegradable punks on a one-way trip anyhow. Instinctively they knew their chances of continuing, their chances of surviving, were better if they stayed in packs.

Brett knew it too. That was why he didn't wait for them behind the door. A ninja less versed in American ways may have thought an ambush perfect to cut down the now cowed enemy, but Brett knew that the hoods' sheer weight of numbers would give the mob mock courage.

He walked quickly down the dark passage until some punks showed up under the stairs to cut him off. Brett looked over his shoulders. More kids were coming from behind. Thankfully the narrow doorway let only a few in at a time.

They were moving slowly, feeling their way in the darkness, since the thick walls cut off any illumination from the street. They peered into the hallway, looking for the telltale gleam of Brett's sword.

Brett could see their knives with no problem, but he had put the samurai blade away. Instead he stood in the hall slipping on his *tekagi,* metal bands that slip over the wrist and knuckles. Also known as shuko, or tiger claws, Brett had made a variation on the classic ninja tool. Instead of just hooked claws on the inside, he had put poison-coated spikes on all sides and on both bands.

Brett stood in the hall as the two groups of punks congregated on both sides of him. Imperceptibly Brett had taken on their posture and tension. As they gathered blindly around him, they were unaware he was moving with them. They were looking for an enemy. Brett displayed his mastery of the *hensu jutsu* art by blending in with the angry throng, making them ignore the dark figure beside them.

He weaved through the milling crowd until he was four men away from the staircase. Then he swung his palm into the face of the punk nearest him. The squishing

99

thunk of the sharp spikes sinking into the man's face brought everyone to attention. They looked all around to locate the source of the attack.

Brett lifted the screaming man up by the hooks and threw him into the center of the hallway. The bloody, blinded hood smashed atop the others, bringing three down with him. The remainder fell upon him and each other, giving the impression that the hall had been gripped with "slam dance" fever.

Brett tore through the trio in between him and the stairs like an attacking animal. His hands clawed through the air in a continuous cycle, shredding the facial flesh of anything in his way. Occasionally one hand would drop out of the circular slashing pattern to knock a knife or crowbar aside. In seconds Brett was out of the hall.

He immediately leaped up to the overhang, his *shuko* biting into the wood. He swung up like a pole-vaulter, his legs clearing the banister and landing quietly on the first-floor landing. The hallway went west, emptying into two rooms. From the lack of shadows, Brett could tell the hallway and the rooms were empty.

He crouched in place, hearing booted feet slamming on the stairs. It sounded as if one smart sheep had left the flock to explore on his own. Foolish fellow. Brett kneeled behind the landing railing, with his sword held in both hands. The lone thug was sailing up the stairs two at a time. He slammed to a halt on the landing. Brett swung the sword like a scythe, cutting the man off just above the knees.

The body dove forward into the wall, blood pumping out of its leg stumps like exhaust out of a jet's engine. Its mouth opened to shout, but the teeth-breaking collision with the wall cut it short. One leg dropped forward with a small thud, the other teetered on the edge of the top stair, balanced on its heel for a second, then toppled over backward and bounced down the stairs like a rubber hose.

The shouts from below revealed that the gang in the narrow hall had finally found out that one of their own had been torn limb from limb. They ran out into the foyer spitting expletives.

"He didn't come out this way!" one cried. "We've been guarding the door the whole time!"

Another spotted the disembodied lower leg. "He's gotta be upstairs!" the punk bellowed and started running up.

"What about the other rooms?" interjected a third.

The footsteps on the stairs stopped abruptly. "You're so smart, you check it," said the man attached to the feet.

"Hey!" the third punk screamed with frightening ferocity. "Fuck you, Washington!"

The one on the steps started to run down to the first floor again. "Your fucking fist is too small!" Washington bawled back, spittle flying from his teeth.

"Hey, asshole!" the man at the door interrupted quickly. "Take care of it later!"

"Fuck you too, man!" the third punk continued, jabbing his finger at the man on the stairs. "I ain't gonna do nothing more with the Bezerkers!"

"Hey," said Washington with dripping sarcasm, "the Red Fists were paid too, man."

"Not enough to work with you, motherfucker."

Washington dove off the stairs with a scream of rage. Brett heard him slam into the third punk with arm-flailing aggression. The rest of the mob began turning in on itself. What remained of Brett's sense of humor urged him to show himself and call out, "Hey, fellow! Remember me?" The majority of his mind, however, digested the new information.

Amazingly the street gangs of New York were working together. They had been paid to trash the Oriental avenger. Brett would have to see if he could temper his attack to leave someone in good enough condition to talk. With

101

a sudden surge of strength, Brett vaulted over the railing and landed amid the struggling gangs. No one heard him drop, and the fight was louder than the shouts of warning coming from the doorman.

Brett walked toward the front-door guards, chopping and spinning as he went. The idiots were too involved with their personal fears and hates to give him any trouble. It was all *kogeki*—sword attack. There was no parry/*uke* or exchange/*kawashi*. The punks fought, the ninja hacked, and the punks fell.

The gang members were just so much swaying wheat to Brett. His lips pulled back from his clenched teeth, and his eye muscles were strained almost as much as his limbs as he swung his blade to meet battling bunches of punks. He cut a swath through them like a harvester through a farm field.

The doorman watched in amazement as the tight-knit groups of fighters were cut apart and then down by the lightning-fast sword of the black-draped demon with the burning grey eyes. In the dusky, murky foyer, the eyes looked like glowing pinpricks floating through the air. The *katana* blade looked like a saber-beam as it strobed across the room spraying crimson wherever it went, never stopping, always twisting in impossible geometric patterns.

The doorman's shouts got louder and more strident as the burning eyes and deadly blade grew ever closer to him. But whenever it seemed some punks would see reason, the sword whirled around, smashing the men aside.

Brett waded through the sea of writhing bodies, the floor growing damp with oozing blood. He kept just ahead of the shallow red river, his legs moving slowly but relentlessly. He slowed, but never stopped. He put one foot in front of the other, pivoted, twisted, spun, feinted, whirled and rolled, but he never stopped.

His arm muscles were beginning to vibrate from the

supreme effort of making every blow a killing one. The sword went through bone, cartilage, muscle, and sinew, chopping them all in half. Whether he smashed into a neck or waist, he buried his blade deep into whatever was near him.

But the object was to keep the sword moving from one corpse to the next body so no one got a chance to fight back or run. By the time the next punk realized the last had been killed, his life would end as well. Whenever possible Brett would kill two with one blow, bringing the *katana* around like a baseball bat, and blasting the two struggling bodies apart.

Before the backswing was even complete, Brett would be directing the momentum in another direction to cut down another punk. It didn't seem possible, but the ninja was killing the entire mob without their knowing it. The remaining men ignored the screams and sounds of falling bodies, concentrating instead on keeping themselves alive, but never expecting a sword instead of a switch-blade.

Incredibly it took only a minute. Brett had moved from the narrow hallway entrance to within five feet of the front door in a little over sixty seconds. The doorman stared in shock at the room behind the black-garbed man. The floor was carpeted in blood and furnished wtih dis-membered torsos. The blade had moved so fast that it was hardly stained.

The doorman shook in place, then raced into the room to his left. Brett slowly followed, maintaining the image of an implacable, passionless, pitiless avenger. Considering his actions, maintaining that image was not hard. The doorman leaped up to the grated window and unraveled the *manriki-gusari* from the links.

He dropped down to the floor in triumph, holding the chain before him with a desperate, knowing smirk. The hooded figure stopped in his tracks when the doorman showed he had the weapon. Inspired by the ninja's sudden show of concern, the doorman moved to the side, then forward, starting to swing the chain.

The ninja moved back. The doorman's smile grew, and he made the *manriki* spin a little faster. He nearly ruined the approach when he slipped on the edge of the beheaded man's pool of blood, but he managed to keep his feet and continue forward.

The ninja moved back into the blood-splattered foyer as the doorman got the chain humming with speed. Brett backed right against the door, taking the moment to check the street. It looked empty, but he sensed there was something out there.

There was another group of punks in the shadows across the street. He could tell by their manner and posture that they were the leaders of the pack—these were the men who let the others do the dirty work. The high-pitched hum of the *manriki* forced Brett's attention back to the doorman. The ninja was about tired of the game.

Brett jerked his body forward and the doorman jerked back in surprise, trying to hurl the chain the way he had seen the ninja do it. The weighted ends spun through the air awkwardly, missed Brett by several feet, wrapped around the doorman, and sunk into his sides.

The doorman struggled in the chain bindings around his arm and tried to force out the spikes that were sticking through his shirt. He moaned and stumbled toward the ninja like a drunken sailor. When it seemed the chain-wrapped dervish would slam into the black-clothed demon, Brett stepped aside, opening the door for him.

The doorman fell through and rolled down the steps, the spikes being pushed in deeper. He slid across the sidewalk, fell over the curb, and came to rest in a heap. In a tribute to his own strength, the doorman wrenched himself up onto his knees and rose unsteadily to his feet. He walked jerkingly forward, screaming into the night. "Parker!" he pleaded, his voice a hoarse, rending bark.

"Parker, please help me! Oh god, Tommy, oh god, please!"

Brett watched in apathetic interest at the pitiful figure wrapped in a chain, blood spreading across his shirt. His yells echoed off the neighboring buildings, the words disappearing in an indifferent night.

The doorman stopped in the middle of Crosby Street, his legs unable to continue any further. "For god's sake. Tommy," the doorman croaked, "do something."

The doorman's chest exploded in a torrent of bullets.

Chapter Ten

Tommy Gun Parker moved out of the shadows across the street. He walked casually forward to survey his handiwork without fear or apparent interest in the building Brett watched from. Parker looked down at the dead doorman with mild interest, then looked over his shoulder and nodded.

Two other thugs raced forward, grabbed the doorman's legs, and dragged him over to the warehouse. Parker watched their progress, waited until they looked back at him, then cocked his head. The two men lifted the doorman and threw him into the dumpster. Brett cringed. He hoped Connie Chesinski was in no shape to get upset at her new companion.

To his surprise the street was completely clear of corpses. The Parker boys had been busy during his street-gang slaughter. The ninja's mind was shaken from those thoughts when Tommy Gun Parker looked back at the silent school-like building.

The man was a physical giant. He must've been at least six feet, six inches tall and two hundred and fifty pounds. His head was big, even for that size. It was covered with a mop of greasy, wavy black and grey hair that hung on his head and chin like stringy moss. It looked like a chunk of granite wedged into a redwood tree trunk.

In his massive hands were two 9mm Ingram MAC-11s complete with silencers. It was no wonder Brett heard only coughing when the doorman's chest was perforated with lead. The large round silencer was bigger than the gun itself.

The gun was a small box with a pistol grip and trigger at the bottom and a tiny barrel at the front. It was only twenty-two centimeters long, but Brett knew what it could do.

It was capable of blasting out one thousand two hundred bullets per minute, or, in more conceivable terms, twenty 9mm/.380 ACP, rounds *every second*. Tommy Gun Parker had two of these monsters, one in each hand. Even from this distance Brett could see how muscular the man's wrists were. And he could see the two rows of ammunition holders strapped to his oil-drum chest and equally wide waist.

"Come on, Tommy," a third man said, running up to his boss who was still looking over the building. "The police'll be here any second."

Parker waved him away. "The police aren't comin' nowhere," he said, his voice a slurred rumble.

"Come on, Tommy," the guy repeated. "Somebody had to hear all the fighting. Somebody must've called the cops."

"Nobody called nobody," Parker maintained. "There wasn't enough noise to get any asshole off his duff."

Brett understood the man's reasoning. The ninja master fought silently, the sound of his victim's yells being nothing unusual in the Manhattan night. And once inside the building, most of the dying cries were cut off by the thick walls. And Lord knows Parker's gun hardly whispered its hail of death.

"Let's go," Parker said to the remaining hoods. He waited until the half-dozen punks passed him in the street before taking up the rear. Each man, as they came, dug a weapon out of his pocket. Brett saw a lone Saturday

Night Special in the hands of what looked like the youngest, and other guns ranging from a Police-issue long-barreled .38 to an Army-issue Colt .45 automatic.

Brett moved back into the house, stepping through the pools of blood without leaving a ripple. When he reached the stairs, he wiped his feet on a dead man's chest. He silently mounted the stairs, trying to fully understand what the hell was going on.

Nelson and company lay in wait for Chesinski. The collected street gangs of New York lay in wait for Nelson. And Tommy Gun Parker lay in wait for the street gangs. Things were coming together very fast and very hard. It seemed that Brett was doing everyone's work for them. And he couldn't help wondering if anyone was laying in wait for Tommy Gun Parker.

Jeff Archer's words ran through Brett's brain. There was a gang war of unprecedented scope going on. Maybe he had stumbled into the night of the long knives for the Manhattan gang hierarchy. Perhaps tonight was the rumble of all rumbles, where the boss man was finally decided.

But the Bezerker gang member had said they all were paid. Who would pay the punks for a rumble tournament? And if it was the Butcher, where was he getting the money and why was he doing it?

Brett had no more time to ponder the questions. The gun-toting crew had pushed open the already ajar door. The kid with the .25 caliber Saturday Night Special revolver was urged to step in first. He bent his knee and planted his foot atop one last remaining *tetsu-bishi*. His foot jerked back up, his eyes widened in surprise, and he fell forward, dead.

Parker immediately surged forward and blanketed the room with MAC-11 fire. Then he returned to his place behind the others, ignoring the young punk they were all staring at. "Go on," he said.

The next man in line pushed the door open completely. The lamplight behind them illuminated the foyer full of hacked corpses. The group stared in wonderment at the bodies, then looked back at Parker's small, still smoking machine.

"Don't be stupid," he said, reading their minds. "They did that to themselves. Get inside." He thought of the dead kid and added, "Watch your step." The men took no chances. They walked across the kid's back.

Parker surveyed the room with respect. He looked up to see the legless corpse at the top of the stairs, sitting with his back to the wall, his eyes wide open—a bleeding harlequin doll in denim and black leather, his head cocked to the side with a stupid expression on his face.

Brett remained in the position he had killed the man from, crouched under the first-landing railing. He decided to wait until the unit broke up to search, so he could pick them off one by one.

But Parker did not split up the unit. The men remained together as they surveyed the downstairs rooms and the narrow hallway. The now five remaining men moved everywhere first, followed by their hulking leader. For Parker it was like a return visit to the pestholes of Vietnam. He walked amid the corpses in the hall, keeping count as he went. His scowl deepened as the body count mounted. But when he got to twenty, his expression changed to a satanic look of anticipation.

"Keep together, boys," he instructed. "And get ready. Shoot at anything that moves as soon as it moves." The boys didn't have to be told twice. Parker directed them to the stairs, and they started slowly up.

Brett waited, figuring the odds. It was possible he could cut them all down, but not before at least one had a chance to fire. And since Parker was the best protected, it was most likely his double-barrel MACs could tear the ninja before his sword could move in.

A fistful of *shuriken*s might even the odds a bit, but Brett doubted he could get out of firing range before the poison took effect. He'd get them, but there was a good chance they'd get him as well. This called for a little strategy, he figured.

Brett reached into his sleeve and slipped one of the *shuriken* out of its pouch strapped to his left forearm. He moved his arm back and threw the thing between the railings supports. It followed Brett's physical instructions perfectly. It invisibly streaked across the room and sank into the open front door with enough power to push it closed.

Almost as soon as the sound of the metal thunking into the wood reached Brett's ears, Parker had whirled around, his MAC spitting fire and metal. The bullet ejection was so rapid, the barrel spouted a bright, thick white bolt of lightning. The door was splattered with steel, turning it into a wooden slice of Swiss cheese.

As all the gunmen spun toward the door, Brett slipped over the railing and dropped to the floor below them. He executed another *soku ho kaiten* sideways roll and came up in a crouch under the stairs.

Two of Parker's men started to run down the stairs to check out the door when Parker swung the MACs back toward his hips. The guns seemed to stick to his waist, leaving his hands free to grab the duo's collars.

"No," he said quietly. "It's nothing— And if it wasn't before, it is now."

He reached back to the homemade wire machine-gun holster and twirled the silenced MACs back into his hands. The men looked in amazement at each other, for the first time realizing they were in way over their heads.

"Just the house settling," Parker soothed with bland conviction. "Keep moving." Slowly, reluctantly, the men continued up the stairs.

Brett listened to their progress above him. He pulled back his other sleeve to expose the *tonki*—poisoned throwing dirks—he had strapped to his right arm. He

111

slipped out four of the five and placed one in each hand. The other two he put in his teeth. He should need no more than that.

Brett pictured it in his mind. First two blades go through the stair bottom and into two men's feet. Just as they are becoming aware of the wounds, the other two go in. As his men dropped around him without apparent cause, the *katana* blade could go all the way up Parker's leg.

Brett prepared himself to act before they could get to the landing. He concentrated, gauging the group's footfalls exactly. His knife-filled fists were up and at the ready, waiting until his instincts cued him. He was concentrating on that so hard, his other senses reported into his brain too late.

He got the green light from his mind just as his ears became aware of the muffled, but distinct, singing voice. "Little Jack Horner sat in a corner, eating his curds and whey . . ."

He couldn't stop the knives. They broke through the wood just as the men surged forward to hunt down the source of the singing. Brett pulled back in time so that Parker didn't see the telltale tips, and the sound of their cutting was drowned out by the twelve heavy feet clamoring up the remainder of the staircase.

"Along came a spider who sat down beside her . . ."

The voice was coming from the first door in the second-floor hallway. The men charged down the corridor as Brett moved out from under the stairs, grabbed the banister, and vaulted to the landing. He sidled over to the small space between where the railing was secured and where the hallway opening began. It blocked him from Parker's view.

"And said, 'What a good boy am I!' "

The men burst into the room. It was a large rundown rehearsal room with a dance bar screwed all the way around the room and broken mirrors covering three walls.

Dusty, ripped mats were covering the floor, and what remained of an upright piano was in the corner. The front wall displayed three tall, barricaded windows, eccentric patterns of streetlight coming through cracks to paint the room in modern art.

Sitting in the middle of the room was Connie Chesinski, playing with a naked Barbie doll with its head missing. She was soaked in rancid liquid and dotted with dried blood. Her hair was matted by dripping crud.

The men stared at the macabre vision. Brett leaned into the hall and threw all four dirks. He was stunned to see Parker watching him instead of looking in the doorway like all the others.

As Brett's arm came down, Parker's gun came up. The ninja pulled his body back as the MAC man pulled the triggers. The wall Brett was behind became confetti, sparks, spitting off the dirks as the 9mm slugs rended them in midair. Only one got through, sinking into the left arm of the man with the .38.

He dropped his gun, grabbed his arm, did a small soft-shoe stumble into the room, and fell against the piano. Connie slapped her hands together in child-like applause as the piano wires were jolted to life.

Brett did not jump back. He was thrown back against the railing, and the building's ancient nails ripped right out of the wall, tearing the railing from its moorings. Brett toppled over, diving headfirst toward the first floor. In a midair turn, he wrenched his body and slapped his feet against the floor just in time. He was flushed with anger and confusion, his normally peaceful demeanor shattered by the turn of events.

Brett felt the fear of failure for the first time since coming to New York. It was a feeling he hadn't had very often in the last ten years, and its very occurrence was enough to scare him even more. There was a chance he might not win. There was a chance he might not kill the gunmen. There was a chance Parker might kill him.

113

Adrenaline flooded his body in uncontrollable torrents. His limbs flailed frantically as if he were trying to climb the floor. He just managed to pull himself around the corner into the right-hand room when Parker appeared on the landing.

More 9mm rounds slammed into the planks and across the wall next to his feet. Brett got completely into the room as the last bullet of the burst ripped through his padded footwear. He felt the sting of a gracing hunk of lead.

That was enough to propel the ninja to his feet. He leaped over the decapitated body—the corpse looking strangely alien to him, as if he hadn't killed it. He landed in the narrow hallway just as Parker ignored the stairs and leaped from the landing.

Brett tried to collect himself in the far corner of the narrow passage as he heard the hulking gunman land. To his shocked chagrin, the man didn't run to the entrance of the right-hand room so the ninja could circle back to the stairs. He moved instead right over to the hallway entrance, barking at his men to cover the room entry.

Brett fell to his face, slithering like a snake as the bullets tore up the narrow corridor. He moved as inconspicuously among the other bodies as he could, but he knew it wasn't good enough. In the flash of the MAC his strobed progress would be all too clear.

Parker instinctively lowered the MAC's muzzle when the light revealed no one standing. He spotted Brett's rippling form a second later. The ninja knew it; he felt the man's eyes on the back of his head. He knew he was dead. The only thing left to do was try and take Parker with him.

Both his hands gripped the samurai hilt in its back scabbard. With a tug he propelled it like a spear directly at the huge killer. It left the ninja's fingers just as he heard the MAC-11 hammer click on an empty chamber.

The gun was empty. Brett's hands were empty. Parker

114

pulled his torso back, the blade just missing his nose. The *katana* sank into the wall behind the gunman all the way to its handle.

Brett swung his feet under him and catapulted himself out of the hallway and into the room over the headless corpse. He moved so fast, the other gunmen hardly saw him. His right hand grabbed *shurikens* off his left arm as he rolled in midair, and he hurled it before he landed.

The four pointed stars spun through the air, thudding into two of the men and scratching the cheek of a third. They died as Brett continued to roll forward, under the gaze of the terrified final man. He moved like a human cannonball until he was right in front of the survivor. Brett heard Parker slam a new magazine into one of the MACs as he grabbed the shaken gunman with the .45 and dragged him into the foyer.

Parker twisted toward them as Brett ran out with his human shield. Parker responded like the man didn't exist. He instantly aimed and pulled the trigger, not even giving the man a chance to get his automatic up. Bullets perforated the already ruined door and punctured the wall on either side. Bullets riddled the last remaining handgun man, making him dance in Brett's grip.

The fucking door was closed. Brett had closed it with his *shuriken*. And he couldn't chance the old bullet-ridden but thick wooden obstruction not giving way if he tried to break through. So he dove into the left-hand room, dropping his crater-covered, gut-spewing shield.

The room was filled with cafeteria tables. Brett up-ended them as he ran down the lentgh of the room, looking for some way out. At the left-hand corner, high up on the wall, he found it.

Brett kicked a table up so that it rested on just two legs and its side lip. That would cover his movements from Parker's eyes. Then he threw another table up against the wall so it looked like a plank on a sheer angle from the floor to the air-conditioning grate. Brett ran

115

back to gain enough momentum. That was when Parker came around the corner.

Brett was ready for him. The last dirk sliced across the room, forcing Parker to fall. The knife missed him, but it gave Brett precious time. He ran right up the angled tabletop and sank his fingers into the grating. If it didn't give on the first tug, the ninja master was dead.

All his strength, all his hate, all his incredible passion coursed through his arm muscles. The grate finally ripped out of the wall.

Even more incredibly Brett kept his footing on the table edge and leaped headfirst into the opening. Parker let loose another MAC blast, shooting sparks off the falling grate. It clattered to the floor, ruined, but Brett was not dead yet.

He had to make a quick choice: up or down. He realized there was only one direction. He planted his hands, knees, and calves against the aluminum pipes and moved upward like a spider.

The next second, Parker did what the ninja expected. The tunnel going down was torn by 9mm shells shot point-blank at the wall. Even if Brett had dropped into the sloping passage, Parker's bullets would have caught him. There was no way the experienced hunter would stick his head in, and the only direction cut off from open view was up. Brett was between floors, and even the MAC couldn't get to him there.

Brett climbed with all his might. Now it was a race to get wherever the tunnel emptied out first. He heard Parker running up the stairs and considered slipping down to the cellar. But there was no guarantee he wouldn't emerge into a furnace. It might have been out of order, but its metal door might have been locked from the outside too.

The upward tunnel leveled off, and Brett pulled himself across with the speed of an olympic swimmer. He saw the end of the tunnel up ahead and went for it with all his might, not even taking the time to pull out his last *tonki*. He slid up to it and smashed the middle with a brutal *fudo ken* immovable first strike.

The grating gave but did not fall off. He struck it again and the obstruction fell away, Brett propelling his body right behind it as if the two were attached. He saw Parker coming through the doorway as he fell behind the rehearsal room's piano.

Parker blasted it. The piano responded by rolling right at him. Once again Parker did the unexpected. He moved forward, grabbed the piano edge with one massive hand, and hurled it aside rather than retreating.

The instrument screamed its resonant last, the wires inside snapping and the rotting wood breaking as the piano rolled end over end. The dissonant music echoed through the room as Parker fired in the direction the upright came from.

The bullets decorated the hardwood floor as mat after mat sailed up into Parker's face. The gunman kept firing, but the mats slammed into him, whipping up a dust storm as he tried to smack them away with one arm. Finally he was forced to use both in order to knock them all aside. When the last one fell, the MAC was back in his hand.

All Parker saw was Connie Chesinski lying on the only mat not thrown, quietly talking to herself while picking at the mat's stuffing. "Jack be nimble . . ."

Parker stood in the doorway, both hands filled with Ingram lead spitters, carefully surveying the room. No crack in the barricade was big enough for Brett to slip through.

"Jack be quick . . ."

Parker carefully checked the ceiling and the way all the mats were lying. He had to be sure Brett wasn't huddled under one of them. Just to be on the safe side, he pumped quick bursts into every hump.

"Jack jump over the candlestick."

117

There was only one thing left. Parker began shooting all the mirrors. Brett quickly pulled the one he was crouched behind over his head and threw it with all his might at the MAC man.

The three-foot wide, three-and-a-half-foot tall hunk of glass was like a giant *shuriken* spinning through the air, glinting whenever some lamp light struck it on its path. Taken by surprise, Parker jerked one gun up but pulled both triggers. The mirror exploded midway between Brett and Parker.

Both men were thrown back by the dozens of whirling shards that splashed out. The ninja catapulted backward while the gunman stumbled back out the door, the schrapnel ripping across his face. Connie Chesinski jerked in place.

That was it, and both men knew it. Brett had nothing left, and Parker hadn't been put out of action. The big man's shoulder collided with the door frame as he surged back into the room. His face was badly cut, and the blood was dripping around his hate filled eyes and onto his clenched teeth.

He glared at Brett in the far corner, making it silently clear that there would be no escape for him. They had battled, and Parker planned to win. Brett looked down the barrel of the huge MAC silencer as the big man raised it to between the ninja's steel grey eyes.

That was when Connie Chesinski threw the small white ball that burst into flame across Parker's chest.

Chapter Eleven

The MAC man ran out the door screaming, his torso covered with liquid fire.

Chesinski was right behind him carrying a small sack out of which she pulled another chalky white, egg-sized orb.

Parker ran into the second room on the floor, racing toward its one window. He threw his huge form at the metal-crossed opening, letting his power and size pull him through. The grating ripped out of the wall, and he crashed onto the sagging fire escape.

Chesinski stood in the doorway of the room and tossed another egg underhand. It went perfectly, dropping out the window and shattering on the fire escape slats. Napalm dripped down like silver foil on a Christmas tree. Spears of fire rained on the falling form of Tommy Gun Parker.

He slipped on the first stairwell, fell down the rest of the steps, and soared over the first-floor railing. He landed back-first on the ground, his chest still burning.

Chesinski saw none of it. She had turned as soon as the second egg was thrown. She skipped back and leaned against the smoking door frame, a third egg in her hand. Her blood-covered, naked chest swelled proudly. The ninja master was standing where she had left him. He carefully noted where her skin was seared by the hot door frame, even though she wasn't blinking an eye.

"The Baker," he suggested softly.

She nodded, smiling. "Good to see you again, whoever you are." She, like everyone else, still thought he was the man who had massacred the Killer B's.

"The torture . . . the phone call to the Oshikatas . . . all bait for me?" Brett asked.

"The whipping, sure," Chesinski shrugged. "I enjoyed that. The phone call, because I thought it would be a kick." She began to toss the egg up and down as if she were George Raft with a coin.

"A bit extreme, don't you think," Brett proposed.

"Hey, baby, I saw what you can do," she said. "Nothing's too good for you."

"I saw what you can do too," he countered, remembering the Oshikatas but nodding his head toward Parker's exit. "Was that trip really necessary?"

Chesinski sniffed. "Hired help. Besides, I wanted you for myself. After all we've been through, I figured it was only right."

"Just another dead Jap," Brett said. "One of many that have been dying around here for no reason at all."

"You ought to know, honey," Chesinski countered. "You've killed enough of them."

"I said, 'for no reason at all,' " Brett reminded her. "I've killed for revenge. What's your excuse?"

Connie C. laughed. She laughed without taking her eyes off his shadowy form. "I like you, baldy. I really do." She started doing all kinds of juggling tricks with the egg. "Don't you read the papers, man? Don't you watch TV? You don't need a reason anymore. I just dig pain, that's all."

Brett shook his head. "Doesn't wash. A one-babe vendetta against society, okay. But an army of street gangs? A professional gunman? Big-time bribes to small-time restaurant owners and two-bit punks? That doesn't make even insane sense."

Chesinski straightened up, grabbing the egg and holding it, her eyes narrowing. "It doesn't have to make sense," she said carefully with contained fury.

Brett paused to see if she were going to follow that up with anything. Silence descended on the room like a shroud. "You're not going to tell me, are you?"

"Tell you what?" Chesinski said with defiance, obviously holding something back.

"Rub a dub dub," Brett said quietly. "Three men in a tub."

"That was just a stupid nursery rhyme," Chesinski said angrily.

"And who do you think they be?"

"It was just a dumb joke! I was sticking it to 'em, that's all!"

"The butcher, the baker, the candlestick maker . . ."

"Shut the fuck up, asshole," she warned, raising the egg.

"Turn them out . . ."

"I said shut up!" she screamed.

"Knaves all . . ."

Connie C. threw the egg. Brett Wallace leaped over it, somersaulted in the air, and kicked her in her enflamed chest as the fireball exploded behind him. She was hurled backward out the door while he scrambled for the open duct high upon the wall.

He skittered down the tube as the girl ran back in the now blazing rehearsal area, her chest bleeding again. She gasped in masochistic enjoyment as she tossed another fireball after the ninja.

Brett reached the downward turn as the egg rolled after him. He slid down like a kid in a playground and vaulted out of the first-floor opening just as it dropped into the cellar.

Fire roared up the tube as Brett continued his slide down the upturned table. He jumped over the shielding table, rolled over another, and ran for the front door.

Chesinski appeared at the first-floor landing as he rounded the corner, another egg in her hand. She hurled it hard overhand as he leaped for the narrow hall. The fireball smashed against the already weakened door, blasting it out into the street with a foundation-shaking boom.

Brett got to his feet beneath the landing and wrapped his hands around the hilt of his *katana*—still stuck in the wall where he had thrown it. The moment his fingers touched the weapon, he felt a surge of calming power. He pulled it out of the wood effortlessly.

Chesinski grinned evilly, expecting him to try escaping down the narrow hall. She kneeled down with another egg in her hand and peered over the landing lip. Instead of seeing a retreating figure, she saw the smiling face of an Occidental man with sandy hair.

Her sadistic expression turned to one of surprise, which deepened infinitely when Brett slammed the sword point through his ceiling, through her floor, into her stomach, and out her back.

The orgiastic combination of pleasure and pain was wiped out by a sensation that went beyond anything she had ever experienced. She gasped in amazement. Her hand opened. The fireball dropped out and fell. Brett caught it casually.

The buildling was on fire, and smoke was already beginning to cover the landing like gaseous steel wool. Chesinski tried to pull herself off the blade. Suddenly the American face was right in front of her. He had done a one-handed chin-up on the landing lip and grabbed a handful of her hair with the other hand. He pulled down, keeping her on the sword.

"Now," he said pleasantly, "where were we?"

*   *   *

The woman who walked into the police headquarters the next day was breathtaking. First of all she was a stunner. Her face was a perfect amalgamation of Occidental and Oriental beauty. Instead of a shallow yellow or chalky white complexion, her skin was a smooth, clear ceramic color. Her lips were full, but not too full to throw off the symmetry of her face. Her eyes were deep with just the right curve of almond shaping.

The body had little to do with the classic oriental structure. She was taller than most Japanese, taller than most women, period. She stood somewhere between five-six and five-seven in her heels. She was shapely more than voluptuous, but everything fit so well and was so sleek, it seemed impossible not to take in her complete form.

The summer dress rippled across her with casual allure, enhancing everything without showing off anything. She seemed to completely accept the way she looked and was totally at peace with it, rather than using it to tease or as a source of egocentric pride. Her manner was assured and serene. In combination with her looks, it created a knockout.

All eyes followed her as she walked through the ancient building. Incredibly there were no catcalls or wolf whistles. The more chauvinistic cops watched her pass in appreciation. The cons looked at her in silence, as if surprised. Later, none of them—neither the cops nor the criminals—would be able to understand why they hadn't acted naturally. They wouldn't be able to pinpoint the reason they hadn't made crude passes or comments.

Rhea Takashi knew. She was *kunoichi*—female ninja. Her father had been a ninja, and at the age of eight she had been promised as a consort to one to be chosen by Master Torii of the Chiba Ninjutsu School. But it was not until seventeen years later, when Master Yamaguchi brought them the tortured man Brett, that her father's offer was accepted.

Her heart melted and was reforged to Brett always. Master Torii was wise in all the ways of life. He knew the soul of the girl and knew it would match perfectly with the obsessed man. Their love was unspoken, but it existed in total reality. It did not need to be spoken. It was. It existed.

Rhea entered the office of the detecive in charge of the Chinatown nightclub investigation. Lieutenant Hansen looked up from his clean desk as she entered. His eyes widened in surprise, not being used to such beauty entering his crime-filled world. Rhea looked at him as well. A big man, he must have been a college athlete. But now his brown hair was thinning, and a slight roll of excess flesh was beginning to creep around his belt. But there was no denying the strength of the muscles beneath his shirt sleeves or the strong conviction in his rugged face.

"Ms. Yamura?" he needlessly inquired, rising. Too many years as a policeman had taught him always to inquire rather than assume.

She nodded. "Lieutenant Hansen," she replied in kind, even though his name was stenciled on the door.

They shook hands, and the detective motioned for her to sit in one of the two chairs in front of his desk. He watched appreciatively as she sat and crossed her long legs. "Now," he said, without referring to a file. "This is about your brother, I believe?"

"Yes," she said calmly. "He's been missing for several days. Have you identified everyone in that nightclub fire?"

"No, not yet," the lieutenant admitted. "What makes you think he might have been in there?"

Rhea waved the question away with a slight arm movement. "That's not important. I want to know what's being done about catching the men who started the fire."

Hansen breathed deeply. Trust even a woman who looked as good as this to be another crank. "I can assure you, Ms. Yamura," he practically sighed, moving behind

124

the desk, "that we are doing everything possible to—"

"What about the reports in the paper today?" she interrupted. "Who are these people taking credit for the fire?"

Hansen sat down and leaned forward. "BLAST," he said, recalling the information. "Another one of those new splinter terrorist groups. The letters of its name stand for the Black Liberation Army for Social Terrorism." He said it flatly, wondering why he was telling the girl all this.

Before he could pursue it further, he heard the beautiful Oriental's next question. "Aren't they taking credit for more than just that firebombing?"

"Yes," the policeman replied. "They claimed responsibility for the blast . . . I mean, explosion that destroyed a building on Crosby Street last night, as well as the bomb planted in Grand Central Station that killed eight commuters a week or so ago."

Hansen was beginning to get nervous. Why was he spilling all this? Normally he would have skirted the issue and redirected the questions toward her. There was something in her ingratiating manner, something in her calm assurance, something resolute in her voice that was almost pulling the information out of his mouth against his will.

Rhea instantly felt his tension. "How awful," she almost gasped, calming him. Her use of *saimin jutsu*—the ninja's nearly hypnotic art of suggestion and imagination—could never be completely reliable with a person as strong-willed as Hansen. Unlike weaker people, who could be kept on the line almost indefinitely, it could be used only on the strong in small doses.

"Please," she said, redirecting it along another path, "I'd like to do something to help. What can I do to assist you?"

"That is very kind," Hansen said, feeling more in control as he stood. "But please, the way you can help us

125

most is by letting us do our work. It is important that you steer clear of things like this. BLAST is extremely dangerous, and only professionals should deal with it."

"Very well, then," Rhea said, also standing. "I am in your debt."

Hansen stared at the majestic woman, momentarily unable to think clearly. The only mental image that got through was the tragic scene of her torn and battered body amid the rubble of a BLAST explosion.

"Ms. Yamura," he said. "Please stay clear of the Mindwich Arcade tonight. We will be investigating reports of the terrorists there tonight, and . . ." For some strange reason he was unable to finish the sentence. He didn't even know why he started it. The possibilities of her being in the vicinity of that dive were a million to one.

"Thank you," she said with a small, but somehow thrilling smile. "I will keep that in mind." She turned and walked to the door. Hansen couldn't bring himself to follow her. She stopped once it was open to look back. "I will check back about my brother."

Hansen nodded dumbly. He had forgotten all about him. Rhea smiled and left the building.

"The building burned to the ground," Brett mused as the car crawled downtown in the always crowded Manhattan traffic. "According to the official police report, all the bodies were burned beyond recognition. No bodies, including the one in the trash bin, were found outside."

"What did Chesinski say?" Archer asked from behind the wheel.

"Not nearly enough," Brett remembered grimly. "She laughed a lot. She said all the contacting was done by phone. Someone called her about her unusual talents and offered a job. She was put on a weekly payroll for terrorist work."

"So the Baker is killed, and the next day BLAST takes her place," Hama summarized.

" 'Hired help,' she said," Brett pondered. "More hired help?"

"Hired by whom?" Rhea said quietly. "To help what? Someone is doing an exceptional job of emasculating a large percentage of New York."

"The butcher, the baker, the candlestick maker," Brett quoted. "Turn them out, knaves all three."

"A knave is a jack in a deck of cards," Hama realized.

"Jack be nimble, Jack be quick," Brett continued.

"Jack jump over the candlestick," Jeff completed. "Co-incidence?"

"Ridiculous," Hama answered. "Nothing like chanting nursery rhymes in the car on the way to a terrorist meeting." He was beginning to act like his old self again.

Brett ruminated on the question in silence. As absurd as it all was, there was nothing funny about the ugly results. The most eccentric, colorful psychotics in the city were being hired to do what they did best to seemingly whoever they wanted. The street gangs were savaging each other like never before, the splinter terrorist groups were dropping bomb after bomb, and the only ones who were suffering were the innocents caught in the middle.

At first it seemed like a good idea to go after the ones doing the destruction, but now that trail had run dry. Between the Baker, Brett, and Parker, all the known operatives had been killed. The Baker had represented the street gang faction, so the Candlestick Maker must represent the terrorist faction. The ninja master had no idea who they might be, and no time to infiltrate. So it was time to become one of the lambs at the slaughter.

The Mindwich Arcade was a monstrous monument to meaningless game playing. It was nestled behind the twin towers of the World Trade Center near Battery Park, filling a building that used to be a produce center. It was long and low with a ceiling crosshatched with girders.

127

The main floor was awash with machines. On the right were the video machines that got harder as the play continued and that the player could never win. The only success there was the length of time played. On the left were the pinball machines, all but a few the worse for wear. They had proven much more difficult to maintain and less profitable than their video counterparts, so they were dying out.

Unable to get rid of them, the arcade managers did their best to keep them running and kept them all against the left wall. There were mechanical machines dating back to the early seventies, solid state machines with digital scoring, wide-bodied units that were introduced in the mid-seventies, and one gigantic machine named Hercules that used a billiard ball instead of a silver pinball.

A wide stairway under a fenced-in shell led to the pool-room downstairs. Thirty tables were there, some still being played by the classic breed of shark. In addition to the grizzled old men in the shiny remnants of suits past, there were the hollow-eyed, sunken-cheeked hoods and pot-bellied, T-shirted bearded bikers, all wearing jackets in the stifling heat.

The joint was jumping with young kids hanging out after school as well as young businessmen stopping by on their way home from work. Workers walked sullenly around with change jangling in their denim aprons. The skee-ball alleys were ignored and silent against the back wall.

Everything moved along as usual until a certain man walked through the front door. He was squat and strong, with yellow skin, slanted eyes, and a bald skull. He wore loose black canvas pants and a loose V-neck pullover shirt that looked like a cross between a Chinese peasant shirt and a Navy uniform.

He walked smoothly across the floor until he bumped into an old bum. The frail man teetered, his plain wood stick sliding across the painted concrete floor. The Oriental grabbed his shoulder to steady him.

"Businessmen playing Pac-Man," Hama said quickly under his breath. "Young guy playing Thunderball."

"More than that," Brett said directly into Hama's ear, his "old man" lips not moving. "Plainclothesmen are crawling all over the place. Get downstairs, quick."

The two men separated without any outward sign of subterfuge. As soon as the Oriental walked down the stairs, eight players and two change men stopped working their respective games and mingled among all the other patrons.

"Police business," they announced, flashing their badges. "Please leave quickly and quietly." The ten detectives moved the others out in a grumbling herd. Brett was forced out with all the others, but he managed to lag behind because of his "infirmary."

"You can't do this to me!" he threatened the undercover cop. "I'm a citizen!"

"Be quiet, pops," the man said. "We're doing this for your own good. There's liable to be some shooting."

Brett stepped onto the sidewalk outside, his mind racing with concern. The man had half said it to get the bum out of the place, but Brett knew the cop honestly expected some gunfire. The ninja turned toward the street in time to see uniformed officers piling out of a van, armed with tear gas and shotguns.

He looked in alarm down the street where Archer was posted. Jeff looked back at him in confusion. This had the earmarks of a full-scale assault, not a preliminary investigation. More cops were keeping the gathering crowd back while the new unit of uniformed men moved in.

Brett signaled Jeff to do the same. Archer was dressed in a store-bought suit for this specific purpose. He marched up to the front door and walked right in, no one thinking he could be anything but another plainclothes cop. The cops turned and started locking the front doors. Jeff quickly joined them, moving to the furthermost door to the left and moving his hands as if he were doing the same.

Instead the door opened out just far enough for Brett to slip in. Straightening, pulling off the worn hat that covered his features, and loosening his facial muscles was enough to smooth out the wrinkles he had created so that he would now be seen as an ill-fitted cop instead of a decrepit bum.

Hama sat on a stool in the corner of the cellar, indifferently watching the pool games. Suddenly one man disentangled himself from a difficult shot and glanced up the stairs.

"Holy shit!" he exclaimed. "The place is full of cops!"

All the men playing, young and old alike, started rushing for the emergency exit across from where Hama was sitting. A man behind the upraised desk that kept tabs on the time played ducked down. Hama slid off his seat and got out of direct line with the door.

The pool player kicked it open to find a line of shotgun-toting uniformed cops waiting for them. They slammed the door shut and started producing weapons from their belts and underarms. As a unit they charged up the steps shooting.

In a split second the pinball parlor and pool hall had turned into a shooting gallery. The man behind the upraised desk reappeared with a pump shotgun. He pointed it at the backs of the men blasting their way up the steps then suddenly swung it toward Hama.

There was no mistaking the look on his face. He wasn't covering the Oriental for later arrest. He was set to blow the yellow man's head off. Hama threw his arms up in what first looked like a pleading gesture. But out of his sleeves poured *metsubushi*—the ninja's own form of mace.

White powder shot out of the tubes wrapped to Hama's arms in a long stream. The chalky dust spread from a thin line to a barreling cloud that totally covered half the room. The deskman blasted into the smoke, dotting the wall with buckshot as Hama slid under the first pool table.

Brett and Jeff heard the booming report of the shotgun blast without seeing any of the pool players fall. Once the players reached the top of the stairs, there would be a point-blank sea of bullets. More uniforms were rushing the front door as Jeff cupped his hands and catapulted Brett to the girders above. The ninja ran along the structural steel using his wooden staff as a balancing rod.

He got to the other side of the entrance and dropped down to the floor again. That was the cue for the two ninja to hurl their own supply of *metsubushi,* covering the upstairs in blinding smoke. Brett then leaped between the cops and the criminals, his hollow staff sprouting a weighted chain. The *shinobi-zue* staff whirled, its lead weight smashing down everyone around him.

He took one spin and then jumped again, this time landing at the bottom of the stairs. The *shinobi-zue* lashed out again, bouncing off the brow of the deskman as Hama's smokescreen began to dissipate. The man's head bounced off the lead ball, then bounced again off the wall. He dropped the shotgun and slid off the seat.

Brett quickly pinpointed his friend. They were the only ones standing in the cellar. "It's a set up!" Hama raged. "The cops're taking no chances. They want everybody dead!"

Brett moved away from the angry man for a second as he heard the telltale woosh of a tear gas cannister being fired down the stairs. He swung the other end of the *shinobe-zue* like a baseball bat going after a wild pitch, catching the speeding cannister in midair. The gas bomb went back the way it came and exploded at its firer's feet.

He quickly moved back to Hama's side, both men crouching by the last row of pool tables. Wallace's mind raced. The whole police force couldn't have been corrupt, and all those IDs couldn't have been faked. Brett had one flashed in his face. Either they were the real McCoys or police headquarters had been ripped off.

For one of the few times in his life as a ninja, he was stymied. Gunfire was crashing upstairs, but Brett wasn't sure what to do. They could try fighting their way out, but that would leave policemen dead. His whole life had been dedicated to defending the innocent, and there would be no way he could rationalize the cops' deaths at his hands.

But he couldn't let them kill him in their eagerness to destroy BLAST either. The whole thing didn't make sense. These guys looked like veteran hoods—more like racketeers than terrorists—but the cops were treating them like the S.L.A.

Whatever the case, he'd have to decide quickly. The smoke was dissipating, and there was no more where that came from. He could see only one way out—they'd have to give up.

They'd march outside with their hands raised high, shouting surrender, and hope Archer and Rhea could spring them later at an opportune time. Brett instructed his *chunin*, and the two moved quickly to the emergency exit. He could only hope that the cops wouldn't gun them down with all the witnesses looking on.

Hama had his hand on the latch when the deskman rose up behind the upraised platform, his sawed-off automatic shotgun pointed at their backs. He had both men in point-blank range.

Brett heard the man pull the trigger and realized it was too late for him to do anything about it. He pushed Hama to one side and dove to the other.

The shot was completely off mark and had ripped the felt off the nearest table, destroying a square yard of green material instead of human flesh. Brett looked up at the deskman. He was still sitting behind the platform

... with most of the top of his head splattered against the Mindwich wall.

Brett's eyes followed the trajectory of the bullet that had killed the deskman. High up on the wall behind the last row of tables was an air-conditioning grate with a jagged hole in it.

As Brett and Hama watched, the grate covering popped off and a policeman catapulted out headfirst. He landed on his shoulders atop a pool table and rolled to a spread-eagled stop across the surface, one foot in the corner pocket.

Following him out of the grate was a massive head. It looked like a marble boulder swathed in bandages. The face looked like a white version of Brett in his black ninja hood, except the mouth in addition to the eyes showed.

"Well, what are you waiting for?" Tommy Gun Parker said. "I got the idea from you."

Brett nodded for Hama to go over.

"Not you," Parker growled. "Your clever friend there. You can get dressed up like a cop. That's what our fuzzy friend is for." He nodded toward the motionless police-man on the tabletop.

Hama looked at his master. "Come on," Parker said. "I haven't got all day." He listened to the gunfire coming from upstairs. "And neither have you. Move it."

Chapter Twelve

"I don't like double crosses," Parker said lightly, putting the Heckler and Koch 770 Sporter rifle back on its rack in his bland, almost windowless van. "And I don't like clients who try to kill me."

The two had crawled through the air-conditioning tunnels until they reached the building next door. From there it was simple to climb out a window, run through an alley, and reach Parker's van on the next block.

Although it was simple on the outside, Parker's wheels were state of the art inside. It was outfitted with the best alarm and communications devices Brett knew of—all hidden behind a false dashboard front. The gun racks too were camouflaged by seemingly natural parts of the van's walls and ceiling.

Even if a thief could get past the safeguards, he wouldn't see anything worth taking at first glance. And if he did a thorough search, he had better be smart enough to leave a man who sported two silenced MAC-11s as well as several other high-powered guns alone.

Parker's story was familiar. He willingly told Brett everything as he drove the van from the arcade site. The ninja watched carefully as they passed the intersection. The doors had been smashed open by uniformed officers outside, the *metsubushi* billowing into the street.

135

The assassin had been called on the telephone. The voice on the other end—male this time—professed an extended knowledge of the hit man's activities and played on his ego. The job was to be massive, befitting his reputation and talents.

One: kill all the street gang members who emerge from the Crosby Street rumble alive. Two: if they failed, kill the oriental avenger who beat them. The method and machinery was left up to Parker, but they did give him one promise and one fail-safe device.

The promise was that no cops would intervene unless the destruction became "extreme." "That was the word they used," Parker contended. " 'Extreme.' " The fail-safe gap was that if it looked like the Oriental avenger was going to defeat him, Parker was empowered to offer the man a job.

"That's when that little bitch let me have it," Parker admitted.

Brett looked at the swathed driver. His face looked bad around the edges of the bandages. The skin was the flaking color of noxious purple, and all his mighty mane of hair was completely gone. As greasy as it looked, it must have gone up like a two-week old Christmas tree.

Parker looked over at his reluctant passenger as he guided the van onto the Avenue of the Americas and headed uptown. The night lights were just beginning to come on in the sweltering heat of nine-o'clock New York. "Since you're still around," the hit man said, "I guess you got the little girl good."

Brett ignored the fishing expedition. "What was the job?"

Parker snorted. "Hey, yeah, sorry about that, but you know, you weren't winning. You were dead meat if that bitch hadn't interfered."

"She beat you," Brett offered. "I beat her. What's the job?"

"Was, pal." Parker grimaced. "Was. Ain't no way

I'm going to work for them anymore. Not after what they done to me." Parker reached across Brett's torso with one hand still on the wheel to grab a vial of tablets from the doorless glove compartment. He popped open the child-proof cap with one thumb and swigged at least three of the pills.

"I've been popping these pain killers all day," he explained, tossing the vial back into the glove compartment, seemingly without looking. "Don't have time to shoot anything up." Brett understood that was "shoot" as in syringe. "Do yourself a favor, pal, don't catch on fire."

"I'll do my best," Brett said drily. He was still unable to shake a grudging respect for the powerful killer. Anybody else would have been writhing in pain at the very least and stone cold dead at the worst. "I still want to hear the offer."

"A steady income," Parker said lightly. "Regular bonuses. Protection. A guy could do worse."

"Could you trust them for it?"

"Obviously not." Parker laughed, giving his bandaged body the once over. "I thought so at first. The cash came on time to where I live."

"Why not just fuck 'em?" Brett asked. "You get plenty work. Why did you need them?"

"They found out my phone number and address. That's no easy shake. If they could do that, they could probably get to me if I refused, so I figured why not? Why not until I got enough info on whoever they were to break free."

Brett had to hand it to the man. He was a cold-blooded murderer, but sometimes so was the ninja master. The big difference was who they chose to kill and why. Other differences included the fact that Parker was a street survivor. He went whatever way the wind blew until he could build a big enough fan. Then he'd turn it on with a vengeance. He did what he had to as long as he had to. But one second after that, watch out.

137

"You got enough info?" Brett asked quietly.

"Enough to go on," Parker replied just as softly, his eyes intent on the road. "How about you?" Still fishing, was Tommy Gun Parker.

"You're the driver," Brett said, leaning back in the seat, eyes veiled. "Take me where you want to go."

Parker shook his head in mild regret. "Better you than your Chinese friend, huh? You gotta learn to give me more credit than that, mister. I can tell a short stocky man from a medium build, even in the dark."

Brett said nothing. They drove the rest of the way in silence. The van finally turned west and drove deep into the West Side. Parker pulled into an alley in the middle of a nondescript city block. He swiveled out of his seat and walked to the rear of the van in a crouch. Brett started pulling off his worn suit, revealing the black uniform underneath.

"So the cops wanted to close in on BLAST today, huh?" Parker said, pushing open a floor compartment and pulling out his MACs. He looked over his shoulder to see Brett looking at him with curiosity. "I been listening to my police band radio," the gunman explained, hooking a thumb at his false-front dashboard. "I know what all the codes mean."

Brett slowly nodded his head and continued to prepare. "Well, BLAST is just a front thought up by the Butcher," Parker continued, strapping on his double-ammo belt. "It was created to flush you out in the open and throw the cops off his trail."

"What is this with all the nursery rhyme garbage?" Brett exclaimed exasperately.

"You got me," Parker admitted. "When I asked what I should call the guy who phoned me, he said 'the Butcher.' Then he laughed. Not a ha-ha sort of laugh, but one of those snorts, as if it was some kind of big joke or something."

"The big joke was those guys back at the arcade," Brett

interjected. "I don't know who they were, but they weren't BLAST."

"Yeah," Parker agreed. "The Butcher is making everybody jack off to his tune."

"So what are we doing here?" Brett inquired, bringing up the *shinobe-zue*.

"The Candlestick Maker is inside," Parker explained. "Along with the rest of the anarchists who really are BLAST."

Brett nodded. He placed both thumbs against the pasted joint of the staff and snapped it open. A pommelless ninja *shinobigatana* rested inside. To Parker it looked like a cane inside a cane. Brett took out what looked like a solid piece of light oak and got up.

"That's it?" Parker said incredulously. Brett nodded. "Well, I don't care if you want to commit suicide, but I don't want you to take me with you!" the gunman vociferated, holding out a Smith and Wesson Model 59 automatic with the fourteen-round clip. "Do everybody a favor and back me up with this, will you?"

Parker fully expected Brett to say something like "You kill your way, and I'll kill mine" and decline, but to his surprise, Brett took the gun and slid it in his waistband. He didn't leave the *shinobigatana* behind, however.

Parker slid the MACs into his homemade holster, feeling strangely comforted that Brett was along. He knew all about the ninja from tales told in Indochina as well as from bad books and movies. In addition, he had seen Brett move on Crosby Street, and as far as he was concerned, Brett had the movie ninjas beat.

The two men left the van by the back door. The vehicle shielded them from the alley's entrance. They were standing before the metal door of a brick building.

"Can you give me a decent idea of what we're walking into?" Brett asked.

"A TV studio," Parker answered. "Fucking guy works

in a TV studio. They make sitcoms and public television shows here. He holds meetings after hours, when the place is empty."

"What does he do?"

"Special effects man. Name of Jack Cannarsa."

Jack jump over the candlestick. It was a joke, but it wasn't a coincidence after all. After a few months in front of the computer monitor Brett might have been able to figure it out. He didn't want to know how many heads Parker had to break to get the information. He pulled on his ninja hood instead.

Parker made quick work of the metal door. One burst from the mouth of the huge MAC silencer pushed the bolt out as if it were hit with a wad of plastic explosive. He shielded the break-in with his large body, his face and bandages flickeringly illuminated by the gun report.

He pushed the door open onto a dimly lit backstage area. The two men moved in, Brett blending with the environment, the *shinobigatana* seeming to float on its own. In the eerie light Parker looked like a cross between the mummy and the invisible man. The duo spread out in an even V, quickly surveying the area.

They had entered the studio behind some flats. Above them was a network of wooden catwalks and a large metal grid upon which large lights could be hung. Only some naked low-watt bulbs screwed into the ceiling above those were on at present.

Brett rounded the corner of the flat to see a simple talk show set-up. There was a pink curtain stretching across one side of the area in front of which singers could do their thing. On three risers, a desk, an easy chair, and a couch were resting.

Three big cameras on wheels were bunched in the opposite corner of the room. Behind them were some simple plastic and steel-tube chairs where a small audience consisting of the show's guests could gather.

Parker came around the other corner of the flat, convinced that the room was empty. He swept his arm toward the exit door directly across from where they had entered, walking steadily toward it. Brett moved cautiously in that direction, his ears buzzing.

The buzzing grew in intensity, but not volume until it reached a peak. Brett took two running steps forward, leaped into the air, and smashed his feet into the middle of Parker's back in a *tobi keri* leaping kick.

Parker was catapulted forward in an unwanted dive. He curled his head down at the last moment so his shoulders smashed into the exit door. He managed to hold onto the MACs as his weight ripped open the door.

Four small charges exploded in the four corners of the room. They were attached to the four corners of the light grid that kept the metal crosshatching secure. The screws and nails spun out of the wall, hunks of concrete raining down on the set. Then the metal ceiling started falling.

"Run!" Parker yelled at the ninja who stood in place, seemingly oblivious to the tons of metal and glass about to smash down. "Run!" the gunman shouted again, the word drowned out as the structure smashed to the floor.

The light plugs were ripped apart, shooting sparks; the plug wires became slashing whips. The large klieg units broke into pieces when they hit the floor, their powerful bulbs exploding. The metal latticework itself slammed to the set with enough weight to smash the desk in half and send the furniture toppling.

A tremendous cloud of dust swelled up, obliterating Parker's view for several moments. When it cleared, Brett was standing exactly where he had been before, exactly in the eye of the maelstrom. He had placed himself in one of the few holes the falling debris afforded and, like Buster Keaton and the famous falling wall gag, let the whole thing collapse around him.

Parker smiled like a shark who had just seen a piranha skin a man in sixteen seconds flat. The shark was still

141

bigger and meaner, but the other fish was still in the same neighborhood—and much faster besides.

Brett nimbly hopped over the destroyed lighting network toward the gunman. As he approached, four men appeared at the opposite ends of the hall Parker was lying in; two on each side. Both duos were shocked to see anyone still alive. The hit man let both MACs slip to the floor in his hands and pulled the triggers. 9mm bullets spat out in both directions, cutting the men down.

They died trying to get away and before they could draw their own weapons. Brett heard more coming from both directions. Parker looked above him, spotting the men's room door on the other side of the hall. He leaped to his feet and lurched toward it. Brett pulled the Smith and Wesson automatic from his waistband and shot a 9mm round between Parker's side and arm and into the handle of the lav door.

The door exploded outward. Parker was thrown back into the studio by the force of the detonation. It wasn't enough to even knock him out, but it would have been more than enough to kill him if he had run into the john.

Parker looked groggily up at the ninja as he caught his breath on the studio floor. As he watched through blurry eyes, the automatic went back into Brett's waistband and the oak cane split into a scabbard and a sword. The *shinobigatana* was, first and foremost, a short, almost straight blade best held with the *gyakute-giri*—reversed-grip sword cut.

Brett held the blade like the murderer held the knife in *Psycho*—blade moving down from the pinky rather than up from the thumb. As the men moved into the room trying to gun Parker down, Brett attacked from the side, slashing with the wicked blade.

He let the first man all the way in and caught the second across the waist. He spun and hacked the first man across the neck from the rear. That blow started the momentum that spun him toward the door again so he could slice up, vertically, across the torso of the third man. The ninja followed that with a fast, savage *zenpo-geri* forward kick that pushed the third man back into the hall, his torso spraying blood like a sprinkler.

"Try doing that with a Smith and Wesson," Parker heard a soft, disembodied voice say.

Brett ran toward the broken talk show desk, motioning with the sword scabbard for Parker to follow. The MAC man covered his back as Brett swept the curtains aside to reveal another door in the wall. "I was hoping there would be another way out," the ninja breathed. "Stand back."

Parker leaned against the wall on one side and Brett took up a position on the other. His leg swung around, kicking down the latch and pushing the door wide open. When nothing happened, Parker jumped through, followed by the black-garbed swordsman.

They were in a small dressing room. Parker turned both his MACs on the closed entrance, making mincemeat of anything that might be behind it. "I'm sick of you doing all the work," he grunted as he kicked open the door. It slammed against a stairway wall, then started to slam back shut. Parker's shoulder bashed it open again, and he ran out on a narrow landing that emptied onto a rectangular stairwell going down.

There were two other doors—one directly opposite the dressing room and one at the bottom of the steps. Three men came around the corner of the first, yelling and pointing their handguns. They never got to fire them, because Parker stood his ground and cut down each one with a smooth, perfectly aimed blast.

"Try doing that with a fucking sword," he grumbled, pounding down the steps. He made it halfway down when a fourth man stuck his arm out from behind the door, pointing a .357 Python revolver right at Parker's back.

Brett pulled the tip of the sword scabbard off. Beneath it was another blade only three inches in length. It looked

143

like a park custodian's garbage picker but worked like a spear when he threw it.

Parker heard it as well, and whirled. His 9mm slugs and Brett's spear hit at the same time. The blade made cold cuts out of the BLASTer's elbow, and the lead made chili of his face.

Parker smirked at Wallace as he moved over and pulled the scabbard-blade free. Rather than trail the MAC man, Brett vaulted over the railing and landed lightly beside the door at the stairwell bottom. Parker was all set to barrel through when Brett motioned him back.

"Watch the top of the stairs," he advised the hit man as he listened and felt the door cautiously. Convinced there was no booby trap on the other side, the duo silently pushed the obstruction aside and walked right into a soap opera.

The door led to the cavernous place where a New York daytime drama was filmed. Rooms were set up all around the massive floor, and many more walls were piled on their side along the walls. The entire area seemed totally empty.

The two men moved in slowly. "Anybody upstairs Cannarsa?" Brett inquired.

"I wouldn't know him if I saw him," Parker answered.

"So we could've killed him already," Brett theorized.

"Could be," Parker agreed. Neither man let down his guard.

Two crashes came from above them. Both men leaped aside as sandbags began dropping like hailstones. Brett spun like a dervish, the sword in one hand and the spear in the other chopping and stabbing a small section clear for him. As the blade sliced open one sandbag, sending the grit spreading out like an umbrella, the spike would sink into another and push it away.

Parker spun, keeping his fingers on both MAC triggers, destroying three bags as they came at him, but missing the fourth. It grazed his back, knocking him forward into the

144

path of two more. Brett appeared in a *tobi keri* leaping kick, knocking one into the other and sending both out of range as his blades cleared the way.

He landed beside Parker, the big man moving so that they stood back to back. The hit man took the moment to add something to their prior conversation. "I don't think we killed him." Then he fanned the ceiling with machine gun bullets. The living room wall behind them jerked up on its mount and toppled over toward the two men.

Parker ran forward and leaped. Brett turned and chopped a slice into the wall as it dropped, pushing through the cut as the wall hit the floor. Parker just made it out from under its shadow as it crashed. He tripped, fell and rolled, barking in sudden pain. The ninja ignored him, knowing the third-degree burns must've been eating him up by then.

Parker dug into his jacket pocket and pulled out the vial of pain killer. His hands were so shaky from the effort of the studio attack and the sudden flare of burning that he wasn't able to pop the cannister open like before. He needed to put his MACs away and go at the thing with both hands. That was when the dogs ran out.

Four Doberman pinschers came growling out from the other end of the studio, their paws unable to gain much purchase on the shiny painted floors. They slid, howling toward the two men: Brett looking the other way, and Parker on his knees with the medicine.

Brett saw them as Parker automatically unsheathed a submachine gun. To him they were only small galloping forms. But Brett's keener eyesight had picked up the bulky coats wrapped around their normally thin stomachs.

"Don't shoot them!" he shouted, but he was too late. Parker's initial burst hit the lead dog head on. The canine squealed, tumbled over his front end, slid across the floor, and exploded.

Parker was sent flying into a pile of flats. The force of the blast knocked Brett over a kitchen table. The Candle-

145

stick Maker had strapped explosives to the guard dogs and sicced them on the two intruders. The *ninja* wouldn't have put it past the bastard to arrange some way the dogs would blow up upon death.

Brett recovered first as Parker fell off the flats. He landed unsteadily on his feet, his knees buckling. From around the corner of a hospital room set another dog scrambled, his teeth bared, his slavering snout aimed at Parker's throat. The hit man raised his gun, but his trigger finger froze. The dog was too close. The explosion would kill him this time. Already, blood from his reopened wounds was beginning to ooze from under his bandages and color the cloth red.

He stared at the oncoming beast in furious frustration just before the ninja spear thunked into the canine's neck. The dog was dying but he wouldn't stop. He kept coming at Parker who swung his silenced MAC like a club across the dog's head. There was a crunching sound as the second animal slammed onto his side and Brett leaped in front of the other two dogs, short sword swinging.

He came in low, cutting open the next dog's chest horizontally between its snout and its legs. He pulled the blade across and then down, cleaving the last mutt's head in two. Before it fell, he slammed his foot under its chest, sending it spinning backwards.

"Come on," he shouted to the dazed Parker. "Let's get out of here." The two were outclassed. There was no way bullets or blades could hurt a man who sent out bombs. They'd have to find him before they could kill him. Brett moved purposefully toward the back wall. The hit man dumped the remainder of the pills down his gullet and followed.

All the doors of the studio were thrown open and what looked like most of Manhattan's minority population had come out shooting. Brett never knew who they were. They looked too old to be more street gangs, and

146

they looked too intense to be people off the streets. It appeared that the Candlestick Maker had a BLAST organization behind him after all.

Both men leaped backward behind the flats. Parker needed no encouragement. His guns started speaking for him immediately. As Brett Wallace was an artist with blades, Tommy Gun Parker was an artist with bullets. He held the six-pound guns in each hand like they were six-shooters and whirled them around like they were party favors.

Brett leaped over his head, landing in front of him in a crouch. Before Parker could say anything, Brett pulled two more 9mm magazines out of the man's holders and flipped back behind him again. "Say when," Brett said in his ear, counting the bullets as they left the weapons.

Parker pressed the clip release on the MAC in his right hand. Brett pulled the empty magazine out and slammed in the new one. He immediately pivoted and did the same for the left one. The MAC fire didn't even pause during the transition.

Parker's magnificent performance pushed the two dozen or so black terrorists into hiding places behind the props. The reveling hit man kept up the pressure as Brett pulled out the Smith and Wesson automatic. The room was lit by twelve ceiling lamps. The ninja had a word for even the most savage and unfair of arts: *hojutsu*—the art of firearms.

Like almost anything else that entered his hands, the gun became an extension of self. He pointed, and the bullet went unerringly. Brett blasted out ten of the studio's lamps when Parker ran out of bullets again. Three BLASTers took the occasion to race forward, trying to get close enough for a clear shot.

Brett had only two bullets left in the gun—he had used one on the lav door upstairs—and Parker knew it. Brett lowered his automatic anyway, waited until the three had

147

stopped some twenty feet in front of them, and shot the dead Doberman pinscher next to the blacks in the stomach.

The dog exploded, killing the terrorists. Parker had reloaded by then and was keeping the others at bay with a wide grin on his face. Brett used the last bullet to knock out the second to the last light. Only a small pool of light was left, illuminating an empty patch of ground. The gunfire died as surely as if the gunpowder dried up. They couldn't see Brett and Parker, but Brett and Parker couldn't see them either.

The set lights came on. All the kitchens, living rooms, bedrooms, hospital rooms, restaurants, and police stations were illuminated with the bright moody light necessary for television cameras.

Parker moved deeper into the shadows against the wall. Brett looked toward the ceiling. The walls for more of the soap opera's sets were hanging there for quick installation. They were attached to a pulley system like the one in most legitimate theaters. Ropes held them up, and the ropes were tied to one wall.

"Stay back," the ninja whispered. *Tanuki gakure jutsu* came into play as Brett climbed the wall like a cat. The *shinobigatana* in his teeth, he found purchase where no one else would, and his digits became claws. He moved into the darkness of the ceiling, grabbed one rope and moved hand over hand to the network of pulley hemp. Balanced on the slack rope as if it were a beam, Brett took the blade in his hand and cut all the hanging flats loose. Like in the days of Jericho, the walls came tumbling down.

The giant set pieces crashed into the standing sets, and they all collapsed atop the BLAST agents. Above the roar of the shattering scenery, Brett could hear the snapping of bones and the crushing of skulls. Parker immediately rose and shot among the toppling scenery, killing anyone who managed to avoid the devastating cave-in.

Within two minutes the fight was over. The soap opera studio was as blood-encrusted as the Crosby Street school building. Brett cut the rope he was standing on and swung down to the wreckage-covered floor just as the door they had originally come through reopened.

Parker turned toward it, his trigger finger tightening. The doorway was riddled with bullets.

"Don't shoot!" screamed a voice. "I give up! I'm coming out!"

The voice was loud, but there was something about it that raised the hairs on the back of Brett's neck.

An obese black man appeared in the doorway, his hands high. He stumbled out, seemingly hard put to stay upright. He took one look at Brett and Parker and ran to the right. Parker's gun barrel tracked him like radar, and his finger tightened. Brett swung the spear, knocking the MAC barrel up. The bullets slammed into the wall over the fat running man's head with a cracking sound.

Parker had had enough. The combination of his pain and the fight had infused him with an anger he had not had before. He swung the other MAC barrel into Brett's chest, knocking him back. "Fuck this, man. He's dead meat."

"I need information," Brett said quickly as the assassin raced after the black.

"Big shit!" Parker screamed in vicious glee, thirsty for the Candlestick Maker's blood.

Brett spun and threw the spear at the last overhead lamp with all his might. It sliced through the bulb and into the socket at the same moment Parker's bullets ripped into the fat black man.

The lights in the studio shorted out as the black man's body burst outward in a torrent of tiny steel balls.

Chapter Thirteen

The 9mm MAC-11 slugs burrowed through the fat man's back, sending him against the wall of a set. Brett turned back as the lights flickered to see Parker turn the corner of the set after the man.

The studio lights died and an eerie glow silhouetted Parker's shape through the canvas flat. Brett saw it all in a shadow show. The black man turned, his middle disintegrated in a torrent of spinning, gut-covered orbs, as if the man had swallowed a pouch of explosive *tetsu-bishi*.

The balls blasted into Parker whose silhouette grew large and then slammed against the flat's opposite side in normal size. As he hit, a splash of blood added a jarring design all around him.

As he slid down the set wall, Brett was already moving. He ran right at the collapsed sets, leaping over piles of rubble, chopping through obstructions, and rolling under twisted beams. There was a window frame in the flat Parker had fallen against. Through it Brett could see the soap opera control room behind a sheet of one-way glass.

He remembered now that one of the bullets he had deflected from the fat man *cracked* against the wall. It had just caught the edge of the window. All along the Candlestick Maker had been controlling the traps from safe inside while he sent out others to die.

Brett realized that the voice that had shouted had an undercurrent of assurance, a firm resonance that did not match up with the frightened, overweight man who appeared. The Candlestick Maker had shouted through the studio's sound system and thrown his last, greatest booby trap out.

The bombs had been strapped to the dogs. This mine was *inside* the fat man. All it took was a miniature explosive and a stomach full of steel balls. No doubt the bomb expert wanted to wait until both avengers were nearby, but Parker's bullets had set off the horrid trap early.

All Brett wanted to do now was kill the Candlestick Maker. He no longer needed information. He knew all there was to know, except why. And if the Baker and Candlestick Maker couldn't or wouldn't have the answer, the Butcher would. And Brett knew just how to find him.

The ninja master leaped into the air, tucked his body into a ball, went right through the small window opening, dropped, grabbed Parker's MAC, rolled and came up firing.

The bullets cut a perforated line through the one-way glass, now exposed by the light inside coming through to the darkened studio. The thin, handsome black inside fell back into a wheeled control chair, his arms crossed in front of his face as lead and glass chips swirled in the control room.

Brett did not stop. His body hit the bullet perforations right at their weakest point. He himself exploded into the booth, right in front of the huddling Candlestick Maker.

The ninja's arm streaked down, the *shinobigatana* shooting point-blank into the black's chest with the power of a cannon. The blade went through the man's body, out the chair back, and into the lighting board behind him. The current coursed through the steel and roasted the bomber's internal organs.

Brett stood on the camera board, watching the Candlestick Maker fry, his body jerking in the chair, sparks spitting from the board, the booth filling with the smell of roasted flesh.

Tommy Gun Parker could smell it from where he lay. All he could see was the ceiling until Brett's face filled his vision. The ninja hood was pulled down off his features. The MAC man lay silent, blinking, until Brett had slipped all the parts of the *shinobigatana* back in place.

"Killed by a fucking 'bouncing betty,'" he said with mirthful, pained irony. "First thing we learned in 'Nam was to steer clear of those motherfuckers."

"The Vietnamese didn't eat them," Brett said flatly. There was no evidence that Parker heard.

"It's just as well," the man chuckled, blood bubbling out of his mouth.

"What?" Brett's voice was emotionless, distant. He did not kneel or offer anything.

"You probably would have killed me anyway," Parker said, then died.

Brett continued to look at the complex, masterful murderer for several more seconds.

"Probably," the ninja agreed.

Lieutenant Hansen loosened his tie. He got up from his desk and walked to the pressed-wood hat rack while rolling down his sleeves. He slipped on his jacket over his shoulder holster and headed for the door. The night shift was ending, and Lieutenant Hansen was looking forward to the new day.

Saturday, he though. Saturday, when he could just get in his car and drive into the sunrise. Saturday; it meant two whole days of relaxation commiserating with the great outdoors. Saturday, the long weekend when he could finally get something done without pathetic paperwork or ridiculous red tape getting in the way.

Lieutenant Steve Hansen closed the door to his office and walked down to the parking lot where his Lincoln

Continental waited. He drove to his apartment on East Sixty-Seventh Street, pressing the button for his automatic garage opener to start. By the time he easily wheeled the power-steering wheel around to the left, the garage door to his townhouse was fully up.

Hansen emerged from the plush, roomy, air-conditioned car as the garage door slowly lowered. He approached the house door as the garage clicked shut and the garage light went off. He twisted the house knob and pulled open the house door.

A woman ran screaming at him from inside, a kitchen knife raised in her fist.

Some men would have frozen, but Hansen was a cop. He had been taught to expect the unexpected. He caught the wrist of the hand holding the long, wicked knife, and twisted. The girl squealed in surprised displeasure, but was forced to drop the blade.

Hansen kept twisting until he had the arm all the way up the girl's back. He forced her against the car, slamming her head on the auto's roof. The light from the house's entry hall shined into the garage, making glistening highlights on the woman's lustrous black hair.

Hansen grabbed a handful of the stuff and pulled Rhea Takashi's head off the Continental's roof.

"You lousy bastard," she swore through bloody lips. "You killed my brother!"

Hansen was shocked into silence. But his police training and macho sensibility instantly clicked on automatic. "Attack me, will you?" he growled with smug superiority. He pulled her wrist down until he could grab her loose arm. With professional aplomb, he held both wrists with one hand and pulled out his omnipresent handcuffs.

"We'll see about that ," he continued while clicking the metal links into place behind her back. Rhea continued to struggle, her shrieks getting louder and louder. Hansen threw her back against the car. He surveyed her for a moment as she shook the hair out of her face and glared

154

back. She tried to run by him, but he caught and threw her back again.

She immediately tried to kick him in the crotch, but he caught that too, letting his hands slip up her trousered leg and linger in *her* crotch while laughing. This time she let loose a full-scale scream right in his ear.

His head snapped away, one hand cupping his wounded orifice. He swung that hand back across Rhea's jaw.

The screams were swallowed up in the stinging slap. The Oriental's head jerked down, her hair making a curtain across it as she gasped in pain. Hansen dug a handkerchief out of his breast pocket, grabbed a handful of hair again, pulled it back, and stuffed the cloth into her open, groaning mouth.

Panicked by the strange intrusion, Rhea started screaming again, only this time the noise was muffled. Hansen bent her back across the car trunk with his hand under her chin while he wrenched his tie off. He then tied it tightly around her head to keep the gag in place. Next he unbuckled his thin leather belt and pulled it free of his pant loops.

Rhea stopped chewing on the cloth, and her eyes widened in shock. That gave the cop enough time to secure the belt just over her knees. He grabbed her around her waist and dragged her inside the townhouse. The girl struggled, her dark pullover coming untucked as Hansen pulled her up the carpeted steps to his living room.

He dropped her on the floor, picked up the phone receiver, and hastily called a 203 area code number. Rhea listened to one side of the conversation as she rolled on the floor, fighting her bonds.

"Hello, Frank, let me talk to Tony. Yeah, I'm sure it is, but this is an emergency, all right? Of course my voice is tight, I told you this was important! All right, sure, just get Tony on the phone.

"Tony? Steve. That Oriental broad is here. Where? Here, at my place, for God's sake! She came at me with a butcher knife! Said I killed her brother. No, of course I didn't let her go. I've got her handcuffed. Here. In the living room. Yeah, she can hear this."

Hansen listened, his face reddening as Tony's voice became an angry buzz on the other end. The cop listened for a while, then quickly put down the phone. He grabbed the girl and carried the sputtering, bucking Oriental into the bedroom. He dropped her on the carpet, pulled another pair of handcuffs out of a dresser drawer, and secured her ankles. He closed the door and went back to the living room phone.

That gave Rhea some time to think. As usual, Brett had been right. The only person who could have made a master arsonist resembled a feeble hooker on the police computer was a cop.

And the only one who could know that the Manhattan drug runners were having a summit meeting at the Mindwich—and convinced the rest of the department that they should be shot on sight—was a cop. A high-ranking cop at City HQ.

Five minutes later that cop returned with a paper bag. Rhea was lying on her back, staring at him with a combination of fear and anger. He rolled her over and secured her hair in a pigtail with some rubber bands. He rolled her back so she could see that he was holding a large kitchen sponge. He pulled his tie down, and she spit out his soaking handkerchief.

"What are you doing?" she said, her voice quaking. "I didn't mean . . . I didn't know . . ."

His face frozen in a cruel scowl, Hansen grabbed her jaw in one hand and stuffed the sponge into her mouth. She howled on the floor, shaking her head, but he kept pushing until it was all the way in. Then he plastered a series of tape pieces across her lips.

Hansen carried the moaning girl down the stairs to the garage. He put her on the floor and opened the car trunk. He reached in and pulled out a length of rope. He pushed her legs back so that her ankles nestled against her rear and her thighs were pushed against her calves. He tied them firmly in place.

Next he wrapped some cord around her neck and tied it to her knees. Finally he bound her arms to her torso. The girl was a sweating ball when Hansen put her in the trunk like a piece of luggage. He slammed it shut, got in the car, and drove out of New York State.

The Connecticut countryside was beautiful, but Rhea didn't get to see it. The Lincoln went through Westchester County, then Greenwich, then Westport tolls along four-lane Interstate 95 until it took exit 18 and transferred to the two-laned Merritt Turnpike.

Hansen went one exit south and started up route 33. He took a right at the sign for Cannon Crossing. Surburbia gave way here for mountainous countryside, which it shared with New York State along its western-most border. This was a hunter's haven, a sportsman's paradise, where anything could be done in the company of only acres and acres of deserted woodland.

The cop followed the winding roads for what seemed like hours, his placid veneer giving way to a mood of excited anticipation the further from Manhattan he got. He was totally alone on the road with his thoughts. And most of his thoughts were about the bundle behind the back seat.

She no longer posed any threat. Tony said that she stopped being a problem when the knife fell out of her hand. All she was now was a magnificently desirable woman. And she was completely his. She was now totally dependent upon him for life and death. The excitement of that thrilled him like nothing else.

His foot pressed down on the accelerator, and the car surged forward.

The Cannon Crossing Gun Club was a sprawling white mansion nestled in the forest like a mythical castle.

The only clear approach to it was from the front, where a long, lush, perfectly manicured lawn stretched on either side of the perfectly graveled driveway.

The only thing that really marred the medieval comparison was the tall wrought-iron spike fence topped with barbed wire, which stretched all the way around the mansion. It cost almost fifty thousand dollars to install, but it was well worth it.

The spikes were fifteen feet tall and were buried eight feet deep. They were evenly spaced six inches apart. And, best of all, the wire on top could be electrified with the flick of a switch. The videotape cameras and the automatic gate openers were extra, but just as necessary.

The gates swung open when Hansen showed his face, and the cop drove all the way to the wide front porch where the board of directors were sitting. The first thing Rhea saw after the trunk hood was lifted was five men. One was Hansen. The man next to him was a wide-faced fellow with a thin nose and lips. He was wearing a light blue button-down shirt and plaid pants.

The man next to him was a shorter, balding man with a light red mustache. The next was a tall, overweight, swarthy man with permanently pursed lips and curly black hair. He was wearing a jogging suit. The man closest to her was a lanky, ruddy-faced man with sparce, whitening hair and a full hunting outfit. Five of the most innocent-looking men she had ever seen.

Rhea wasn't sure what to expect, but it wasn't anything this frighteningly normal. Her feeling showed on her face, because the ruddy faced man looked back with a wide smile. "She lives up to your description, Steve," Anthony B. Merritt, attorney at law, reported. He nodded to the others. "Take her inside."

The man with the red mustache moved up. "Wouldn't it be best to take her around back?" Frank Sherman, Wall Street stockbroker, asked.

Merritt chuckled. "Relax," he said, putting a hand on

Paul's shoulder. "How long will it take you to learn that no one, absolutely no one can see us from the road?" He looked at the others and nodded his head toward the mansion.

Paul Fuller, advertising executive and gun club driver, reached in and lifted the girl with the help of Dr. David Worley, the man in the plaid pants. They carried her inside, where Meritt cut away most of her bonds, leaving the wrist cuffs intact. The last to go was the tape, which Tony tore from her mouth.

Rhea was already screaming before the sponge was completely out of her mouth. The five men smiled at each other as the sound echoed up through the large, sumptuously decorated foyer. "Please," said Merritt, "feel free to scream as much as you'd like. Even if there were someone within miles around to hear you, the house is completely soundproof."

"Who are you people?" Rhea exclaimed. "What are you doing to me?"

"The question, I think," Merritt said mellifluously back, "is what are you doing to us? You accused Mr. Hansen here of killing your brother."

Rhea looked with fear at the cop, then around at the other interested men. She tried to move back out of Fuller's grip, her tearing eyes blinking at the lawyer. "What do you do here?" she asked in a small voice.

"Why, we all live here," Merritt said. "We have all the comforts of home. We have miles of land, streams, and lakes. There is a pool out back and a wine cellar downstairs."

"You all . . . ," Rhea stuttered, trying to understand. "You all live here?"

"Yes," Merritt said politely. "David here moved in after a gang beat his wife and four-year-old daughter to death just to get her purse." Rhea looked into Worley's dull, sad eyes and his frozen smile.

"Paul came over after his parents died in a plane crash.

159

A terrorist group had planted a bomb in their Air Bermuda jet." Fuller's face was sullen and veiled. "Frank decided to join us when his wife was kidnapped by a street gang. They drove around the streets, gang raping her for hours. She had to be put in a sanitarium after that. Poor woman. Died last year, didn't she, Frank?"

"Y-yes," Sherman choked. "Last December."

Rhea looked into Merritt's face, a deep horror etching her features. An honest horror. But he continued undaunted with the same civilized manner and tone. "Steve, of course, is our most recent convert." Merritt clapped his hand around the detective's shoulders.

The lawyer said no more. Unable to contain herself, Rhea blurted. "What happened?"

"Nothing *happened*," Hansen said with bitter sarcasm. "What has to happen for a man to realize just how sick and disgusting the city has gotten. How many battered children, raped women, and mutilated corpses does it take for something to happen?" He struck the last word with a verbal hammer.

"Now, Steve," Merritt soothed. "There's no need for that sort of thing. I think Ms. . . . Yamura, is it?" Rhea remained motionless, shivering. Hansen nodded. "I think Ms. Yamura is beginning to understand the arrangement."

The conversation was interrupted by a distant bell. "The front gate!" Sherman exclaimed.

"Now, calm yourself, Frank," Merritt said quickly. "It's probably nothing. Steve, why don't you take our esteemed guest downstairs?" The others moved into another room while Hansen took Rhea by the elbow and led her to a door on the right side of a wide, ornate staircase leading up to a beautiful picture window that overlooked a magnificent view of the mountains beyond.

The door led to a spiral staircase, which the cop forced Rhea to go down first. It emptied into a two-lane bowling alley. He dragged her across that, her reluctant feet slid-

160

ing across the shellacked surface in her fashionable shoes. She tried jolting her arm out from his fingers, but his grip was firm.

They next passed through a luxurious bath area with a recessed grotto complete with redwood tub and a sand-blasted plexiglas circular shower stall. Just as they were leaving that room, a chill went down Rhea's spine. She saw fur- and velvet-lined thongs on the ceiling, wall, and steps of the shower and whirlpool bath. A person could either rest or be secured in there.

Her discovery only kept her from looking in the new room Hansen was pulling her into. When she turned, she could not help but gasp. It was a carpeted, padded, elegant gymnasium. But the equipment was for only one type of exercise. There were rings attached to the ceiling and floor. Only, the rings didn't consist of a wooden circle, but a pair of leather cuffs. The floor rings were separated by a space of four feet.

There was a loveseat that did not consist of an S-shaped sofa, but of metal tubes designed to make anyone lying across the seat vulnerable to assault. There was a phallic pole secured to the floor, with straps lying on all sides. There was a deep, plush brass bed with more straps attached to the golden bars at the head and baseboard.

Finally there was a hanging array of straps. These straps were connected to the ceiling and floor. They strapped to wrists, arms, neck, waist, thighs, and ankles. When they were attached, a person would hover spread-eagled in midair. Rhea knew, because the body of a young, naked black girl was already tied there.

Hansen pushed her into the room wordlessly. She couldn't be sure, but Rhea thought she saw an expression of regret pass over his face as he closed the door behind him. Rhea looked in tragic bewilderment at the elegant sexual torture chamber. She looked at the dead black girl hanging in the straps.

161

As she did, her clenched fist loosened. A soiled, wrinkled hair ribbon she had found in the trunk slipped through her fingers and fell to the padded floor.

Merritt answered the gate bell personally. He sat in the room off the foyer, in the padded chair in front of the antique rolltop desk, and operated the videotape unit and microphone. The early morning sunshine poured into the airy, high-ceilinged rooms from the voluptuous curtains.

"Who is it?" he asked of the young stranger standing next to the van.

"Tommy Gun Parker," the thin, wiry, brown-haired man said. "And I've got a present for you."

Chapter Fourteen

The Cannon Crossing Gun Club had little choice but to let him in.

If they sent him away, he might go right to the police with a pretty little story. Maybe he couldn't prove it, but he could attract enough attention to the place to make their lives hell. The questions would range from the serious allegations he could bring to ones as simple, but as potentially embarrassing as: "why don't you let anyone else join this so-called Gun Club?"

So they made sure he wasn't carrying any weapons by having him take off his shirt, pull up his pant legs, and open the van for video inspection. When they saw what was inside, they hastily opened the gates, and the man who was calling himself Tommy Gun Parker drove up to the front door.

Dr. David Worley was the first one out. He met the young man at the bottom of the stairs, and the two moved around to the van's back door. The kid pulled it open with a flourish and said, "Ta-da!"

Inside was the corpse of the man who had killed the Killer B's.

Worley did a thorough examination on the stocky, bald Oriental. He emerged from the van a minute later, rubbing his hands on his plaid pants. "He's dead, all right. No pulse, no heartbeat, no respiration."

"What did he die of?" Frank wondered aloud. "There's not a mark on him."

"Didn't you shoot him?" Merritt asked civilly. "That is, after all, your speciality."

"Naw, I didn't shoot him," Jeff Archer stressed. "I knew the guy. We were drinking. I just couldn't pull a gun on a buddy. I drugged him."

"Poisoned him," Merritt suggested.

"Poisoned, o.d., drugged, sure," Archer replied. "Whatever you want to call it."

"Doctor," the lawyer called, "did you check the pupils?"

"Of course," Worley said with professional pride. "Dilated."

Merritt cleared his throat. "Well then, Mr. Parker, to what do we owe this pleasant surprise?"

"I'm no idiot," he said, scowling. "I saw what was happening. After that broad tried to kill me, I figured either I could run for the rest of my life from you guys or . . ." He thought about it a few seconds, then hooked a thumb back toward the motionless body of Hama. "Or I could give you guys a sign of my good faith."

"How did you find us?" Sherman said nervously.

Archer looked at him sagely, with one eye narrowed and a big grin across his face. "If you could find me, I could find you. We professionals have got to have some business secrets. If you tell me, I'll return the favor."

Sherman looked like he would rather court a rattlesnake. Worley looked diffidently at the corpse. Fuller seemed to stare right through the slight gunman. Only Merritt maintained a sophisticated pose.

"A capital idea, I'd say," he exclaimed. "Mr. Parker, would you mind stepping inside while we tend to your . . . . uh, gift? We can share a little wine and talk about the future."

Archer was led into the drawing room, an impressive library with a monumental fireplace over which an imposing painting of a judicious-looking man lorded over the Persian rug, the antique oak tables, and the crystal-covered shelves filled with books, and the enormous desk in the corner.

"My father," Merritt said, pouring a delicate glass of deep red liquid from a crystal decanter. He didn't even have to see if Archer was looking at the portrait. It overwhelmed everything else in the room. "He was a judge." The attorney handed the glass to the gunman. He smelled the wine's bouquet while Archer chugged it in one gulp. "He was killed when a bomb blew up his car." Merritt took a delicate sip.

"Oh, yeah?" Archer said. "That's too bad." He looked around and decided to sit in an armchair that faced the desk. The lawyer circled the desk and carefully sat down himself.

"I must admit you surprised me, Mr. Parker," he said. "From what I've heard, I was expecting a far more imposing figure."

"Oh, yeah?" Archer repeated. "Well, from what I heard, I was expecting a much more imposing figure myself. I mean, who would've thought a guy who calls himself the Butcher would live in a place like this?" Archer opened his arms to lightly encompass the entire mansion.

Merritt smiled and looked down at his hands on the desktop. "Yes, and I wear that name proudly. It was given to me by a great worker for our cause. I will always wear it proudly, so long as it remains necessary."

"Your cause?" Archer asked with incredulous humor. "What's your cause? To kill everybody in New York?"

Merritt was undaunted. He shrugged lightly. "If that's what it takes."

At that moment Lieutenant Hansen entered the room. He strode over to the desk, obviously incensed. "What is

165

this about Tommy Gun Parker?" he asked. "How the hell did he find us?" He glanced at the man in the chair and did a double take. "That's not Parker!" he yelled, scrambling for the gun in his shoulder holster.

"Yes, I know," Merritt soothed, his hand touching Hansen's arm. "Calm down, Steve." He looked at Archer. "I hope you will excuse the lieutenant. But you understand, don't you? A complete stranger drives up with a dead man in the back of his van—a corpse who fits the description of a man we've been trying to capture for days."

"Capture?" Archer echoed.

"Of course!" Merritt announced. "This man was the finest warrior we had ever heard of. Alone and practically unarmed, he decimated two of the most vicious street gangs single-handedly! Naturally we wanted to convert him to our cause."

"He's dead now," Archer said hollowly. "I killed him. So convert me."

Merritt seemed to consider it. "Very well. We would like to pay you ten thousand dollars a month to kill as many evil people as you are able. For every year you survive, there is a fifty thousand dollar bonus and a raise to twice the monthly amount."

"Don't you want to know who I am?" Archer asked, bemused.

"It makes no difference," Merritt countered. "Do you want to tell me?"

The ensuing silence hung in the room like a shroud. "I don't understand," Archer finally said in total honesty. "The only reason this warrior came here in the first place was to take revenge for a friend who was murdered. An innocent young girl. And now you want to pay me to kill more?"

"Not innocents!" Hansen stressed.

Merritt sighed. "It is regrettable. We started by doing all this ourselves. We realized that the only way to save the city was by eliminating all the . . . shall we say, undesirables. We had no way of knowing the deaths of some blacks and Puerto Ricans would incite the minority street gangs to war. It seemed they thought these deaths were due to their rivals."

"Unfortunately that only made things worse," Merritt continued. "The splinter terrorist organizations saw these rampant murders of minorities as a genocidal plan by the intelligence agencies of the Government. They drew attention to their theory by planting bombs. Naturally we had to take steps to rectify this matter without endangering the overall program."

It was coming together in Archer's mind. Madness upon madness was piled atop of itself until there was no sanity anywhere.

"So you paid them to kill more people?" Archer asked incredulously.

"We brought them out in the open!" Hansen seethed. "We had to prove to the people of the city just how evil and dangerous these people were. We had to make them do something! We had to force them to wake up!"

"How?" Archer barked angrily. "By killing the parents of one of your victims? By burning them alive?"

Merritt raised his hands and pursed his mouth. He made little shushing noises and small calming motions with his hands. "That was terrible," he agreed. "The person who did that saw the Oriental warrior as an evil person. She only thought she was protecting the program."

Archer was stunned. He sat back, his mouth open in amazement. "Now let me get this straight," he hesitantly started. "You hire the most homicidally psychotic people in New York to continue killing?"

"To wake the people up!" Hansen maintained.

Merritt quieted him. "That is essentially correct. We discover the people most suitable for our needs through the knowledge and experience of Lieutenant Hansen and contact them thusly."

167

Archer shook his head, as if to dislodge the parasite-like thoughts that clung to his face. "Homicidal psychotics," he mumbled.

A look of confusion crossed the attorney's face. "Why the stunned expression, sir?" he asked gently. "What, after all, are you?"

Archer couldn't speak. He looked away, trying to gather his thoughts. In that moment Merritt reached under the desk and pulled the trigger of the Winchester Model 1200 Riot Gun that hung there.

The outside wall of the desk splintered into shards, and Archer's middle was torn by tens of spinning pellets. Blood splattered the back of the cushioned chair as it toppled over.

The lawyer hauled the riot gun out of its desk hanger, his civilized veneer completely ripped away. This was the man who beat Tamara Anderson to death in the back of Hansen's Lincoln Continental.

"Sherman!" he bellowed as he stalked out in the foyer, the twelve-gauge shotgun still smoking. "Shoot the body in the van!" Worley and Fuller came running in response to the shot.

"But he's dead," the doctor replied.

"I said *shoot him!*" Merrit screamed, throwing the 1200 over the men's heads into the arms of their resident marksman.

Sherman caught the gun nimbly, spun it like a military parade performer, and ran to the rear of the van. He aimed it right at Hama's head.

A sword shot out from under the van's carriage, cutting Frank Sherman off at the ankles.

The red-haired marksman fell off his feet, the shotgun blast ripping into the vehicle's ceiling, opening it like a soda can. He cried out in fear when he found he couldn't get his footing on the driveway.

Brett Wallace came out from under the van, the black

katana in one hand, the *wakizashi* in the other. He rose up on the grass seemingly without using his legs. He just grew into their vision. All four men inside saw the look on his face.

"Slam the door!" Merritt yelled, already running into the gun room. "Lock it! Bolt it!"

Hansen needed no encouragement. The door swung closed, the cop's muscular hands swatting the locks into place. As his hand twisted the dead bolt, a sword point sliced right through the door and went deep into his left arm. The cop groaned and pulled back, blood drooling out as the blade receded.

He turned and fell to one knee as the others moved forward to support him. They were driven back in a flurry of legs as the sword hacked into the door to the right of the locks.

Merritt came rushing back with four weapons. He gave the Heckler and Koch 93 Assault Rifle to Paul Fuller, the Armalite AR-180 to Dave Morley, the Iver Johnson Super Enforcer to the wounded Hansen, and kept the Dan Wesson .44 Magnum for himself.

The sword chopped through the door directly above the locks.

"As soon as the sword appears again," Merritt whispered, "fire. He's got to be right behind it."

The men waited in tense silence as the blade ripped out of sight with a warping wrench. After a pause of three seconds, the sword smashed into the wood below the locks.

The .223, .30, and .44 caliber bullets plowed into the door, sending smoking and wood shrapnel everywhere. The Armalite, 93, and Super Enforcer spit out lead in rapid succession, obliterating the door from sight.

After another second the torrent of shattering gunfire stopped, its echo swallowed up by the house. The men stared through the gunpowder mist at the motionless sword tip still wedged in the door. A moment later blood began to seep down its length, bunched in large drops on its tip, and splattered to the floor.

The delirious Hansen smiled. The doctor breathed out in relief. Fuller's expression remained blank, and Merritt's did not change. The men slowly moved toward the door, guns still at the ready.

They stopped in front of it, unsure as to what to do next. The blood meanwhile had begun to seep in under the bottom crack. Fuller suddenly reached out, undid the lock, grabbed the knob, twisted, and swung it open.

Frank Sherman was nailed to the other side by a *wakizashi* that went all the way through him and under the door's locks.

Brett Wallace came roaring out of the side room and brought the *katana* down diagonally across Dr. Worly's head.

While they had been shooting, Brett had broken open one windowpane and let himself in.

Merritt, Sherman, and Hansen went flailing back as the ninja master cut off Worley's entire face. From the neck back was open skull—guts, brains, and blood coursing out. The front flopped to the floor, the head looking like a fallen Dave Worley mask. As it settled, the ears drifted back out of the sockets.

Fuller was too terrified to shoot. His normally blank expression was twisted into a permanent visage of panic as the others ran in opposite directions. The driver hesitated for one second too long. As he turned to run, Brett hurled the sword with a scream.

The blade entered Fuller's ear and came out his left eye to sink into the wall behind him.

Brett wrenched the *wakizashi* out of the door, letting Sherman's shattered corpse fall, and raced after Hansen. The cop reached the top of the stairs as Merritt practically fell down the steps to the cellar.

Brett reached the bottom stair as the cop turned before

170

the picture window and fired the Iver Johnson machine pistol.

Time seemed to stop. The last two bullets in the nearly spent fifteen-round clip streaked unerringly at Brett's head. Whichever way he ducked, one of the two bullets was bound to hit him.

Hansen knew it. All his experience told him the shots were perfect. It was check and mate.

Brett ducked to the right. His blades swung across his face to the left. One bullet just missed his left shoulder, ripping off a piece of black tunic. The other bullet smashed into the samurai blades.

It ricocheted off the hard and soft five thousand–folded metal. Instead of tearing off Brett's head, it streaked across his cheek, leaving a shallow channel.

Time caught up with the corrupt policeman. Brett jerked in place, the lead tearing off his flesh. He instantly dispelled the shock, feeling a curtain of blood ooze down his cheek. He smiled. The pain felt good.

Both swords left his hands. They slammed into Hansen's eyes and erupted out the back of his head. The cop flew backward through the picture window.

Brett was through the door before the man landed outside.

Merritt burst into the sex room. Rhea came at him from the side. Incredibly fast, the lawyer pulled the .44 in that direction and shot her point-blank. The woman vaulted back, her shoulder shattered by the high-powered round. Merritt was on her instantaneously.

When Brett entered, the .44 was pressed against her chin. Merritt was crouching behind her, one arm around her waist, her blood soaking his sleeve.

"What are you going to do now, ninja?" the lawyer taunted. "How can your swords help you now?"

The ninja master stood tall in the darkened doorway, the eerie light of the bath outlining his hooded skull. "I have thrown away my swords," he said, his voice coming from everywhere but his mouth. "The swords are the soul of the samurai. I have given up my soul to kill you."

"Oh you have, have you?" the lawyer laughed. "Your bullshit doesn't scare me, asshole!"

The gun left Rhea's chin to point at Brett's head. Merritt pulled the trigger. Brett's head disappeared in a flash of muzzle fire. Hunks of guts and skull splattered across the padded walls and floors.

Even Merritt was amazed. He hadn't expected the master killer to die so easily. He felt a wave of relief wash over him. Then he looked down. The point of a *shuriken* was embedded in his arm.

Brett Wallace appeared in the doorway again. Merritt tried to bring the heavy revolver up, but it would not rise. The ninja master walked forward, gripped the chamber, and twisted it so the man's forefinger was broken.

Merritt fell back to the mat on one shoulder. "You . . . died," he said slowly, his voice thickening.

"Idiot," Brett said, holding the wounded girl in his arms. "I had to make sure no one told you what Parker looked like. That was his head."

Merritt chuckled. "At least . . . at least I will die peacefully."

Somewhere between life and death, the attorney heard Brett's words: "Don't count on it."

Epilogue

Anthony Merritt awoke next to the swimming pool, staring into the bloated, purple face of Tamara Anderson.

He tried to push her away, but his hands would not move. He looked around wildly and saw a medium-sized man with grey eyes and sandy hair standing behind him.

"Ninja," the attorney breathed.

"Back from the dead again," Brett said.

"But not for long, I gather," Merritt replied lightly, jerking his head to the black girl roped to him.

Brett didn't answer that. Instead he walked around the captive lawyer. "The cords and handcuffs that bind you are the ones with which the Japanese woman was tied," he explained. "The girl represents your hate for certain individuals, which became twisted hate for the entire race, and then hate for everyone but yourself."

"Oh, Christ," the lawyer moaned with impatience. "Get it over with."

Brett ignored him. "The bald warrior has risen from his own death after the trance that slowed his metabolism was broken. He has stayed with the woman and the young man. Both will recover. Your buckshot was slowed by the heavy oak desk, and the shoulder can be repaired."

Brett stopped to look at the sunset. It painted the beautiful Connecticut sky in swashes of gold and blue. The ninja master suddenly longed to be part of them—a horrible deep longing—away from the life that created the man bound beside him.

"I came back just to be here now," he told him. "With you."

"How touching," the lawyer sneered.

Brett reached under Merritt and pushed him and the girl tied to him into the pool. The man fully expected to sink down, frustrating his enemy again with a simple, fairly quick death. To his surprise, Brett had emptied the pool so that Merritt stood with his nose just over the waterline. He sputtered and struggled to turn toward the ninja. Once he locked eyes, he smiled and let the girl drag him under.

He managed to remain under for forty-five seconds—until the knowledge that he could stand up if he wanted to and the pressure in his brain became too much. He pushed his head up over the surface again, gasping for breath.

Brett did not say anything. He could have commented on just how hard it was to willingly die, but he knew that would only strengthen Merritt's resolve to die quickly.

Instead Brett lifted Connie Chesinski's bag of fireballs off a lounge chair. He held up an egg. He let it slip out of his fingers. It cracked on the edge of the pool, liquid flame spreading across the water's surface.

Merritt instantly ducked down again. He stayed there for thirty seconds this time, until he saw a hole in the flame above him. He emerged to breathe again. "I know what you're doing!" he yelled. "I know what you're *trying* to do," he corrected himself. "And it won't work!"

"Show me," the ninja master said, and dropped another egg.

Merritt tried. He desperately tried. Time and time again he told his throat to swallow water. Time and time again he instructed his lungs to fill. Time and time again he told his body to sink. Time and time again he looked for a break in the fire and came up.

174

Brett looked down at the man with something resembling pity. A man driven insane by the insanity around him is no less insane. He didn't deserve sympathy. He deserved a death befitting his life.

Brett knew his *saimin jutsu* well. Now he knew it too well for his liking. No man who felt the godlike power of total control over hundreds, perhaps thousands of lives could give up his own easily. There was no telling how many deaths Merritt had actually been responsible for. More's the horror.

"You cannot make me ashamed!" Merritt sputtered in defiance. "The only difference between you and me is our perception of evil! I will die without shame!"

"Don't be ashamed," Brett said quietly, his soul blackened. "Just die."

It took an hour and twenty-one minutes.

EXCITING ADVENTURE SERIES
MEN OF ACTION BOOKS